a novel

by

Lorraine Duffy Merkl

The Vineyard Press
Port Jefferson, N.Y.

*first edition*

The Vineyard Press, Ltd
106 Vineyard Place
Port Jefferson, NY 11777

ISBN: 1-930067-70-4

Cover design: David Cohen

For Neil

1981: Brooklyn, New York. You had me *before* hello.

# Acknowledgements

"Thank you" just doesn't seem enough for ...
Frances Buzzeo and Lucille Bellwood, Maddalena DeMaria, everyone at The Vineyard Press, Evelyn Sottle, Mike and Rose Buzzeo, Cecile Lozano, Neil and Jessica Merkl, as well as Tom, Steve, Dan, Andrew, Eve and Mary, plus Kathy, Mike, Maureen and Joi, my parents, Jack and Angelina Duffy, and, of course, Luke and Meghan.

A special shout out to the professionals who have supported my writing: Christopher Moore, Charlotte Eichna, Paula Brancato, and Martin Shephard.

"No matter what diet I was ever on or how much weight I ever dropped, the one thing I never seemed to lose was the big, boisterous, body-jiggling laugh of a fat chick."

--from *Fat Chick* by Lorraine Duffy Merkl

## Prologue

I was finally a "fat cat" ruling my world from a fully reclining royal blue velour aisle seat. It was my first ever ride on a corporate jet, courtesy of *TREND* Magazine, prominent client of one of New York's hottest boutique agencies, Image Advertising.

As the newly minted Image Vice President Account Supervisor, it was my job to oversee their new major ad campaign. I had been in advertising a mere seven years and I was still under thirty. I had never looked better. Felt better. Been better. Unlike most everyone else in The Big Apple, I didn't have a shrink, but if I had had one, I believe he/she would have told me I had a goddess complex, which was OK considering I actually did think that I was a goddess. Finally.

It's funny, actually stupid, that all the self-help books and women's magazines tell you to, "find your inner goddess," "be the goddess you know you are," "act like the goddess you want to be seen as," blah blah blah. Then when you accomplish this, everyone thinks you're conceited. I didn't care. I didn't care what anyone thought anymore, except the consumers who would be persuaded by our brilliant ad concept for the foremost bible on what's in style.

Each ad would be a "behind the scenes" shot to show that the glamour of *TREND* was not just on its glossy pages. We were on the way to Miami to capture the rigors that go into a South Beach fashion shoot;

flying to Paris to shoot *TREND*'s editor-in-chief meeting with some new designer on the way to being the next big thing; on to Australia to shoot the photographer who was shooting "Great Places to Go in Sydney" for the magazine's travel section; next we were to follow a fashion editor to Los Angeles to hunt down the best vintage stores on the west coast; then on to the tiny community of Arroyo Seco, just outside the tony mountain town of Taos, New Mexico to get candid shots of a journalist interviewing Julia Roberts at her two-million dollar, sprawling forty-acre ranch.

Besides me, our flying fashion show took off with the agency's Creative Director, Byron Jackson, *TREND* editors and assistants, the ad campaign photographer, the fashion photographer and a bevy of established supermodels who were coming out of retirement, taking a break from their new television careers or putting aside their hatred for the business, simply because *TREND* had come a-calling.

I would have to remind myself to mentally document everything so that Kim, my model-worshipping pal from the gym, could live vicariously.

"That's a great jacket," Gisele mentioned to me at 30,000 feet.

Yes it was. Black linen, peplum cut with etched black buttons and black beads embroidered on the collar. It looked vintage, but was actually brand spankin' new from Anthropologie on lower Fifth.

"Thanks," I said.

"Could I try it on?"

*Like I would say no?*

After she did, Gisele conceded, "It looks better on you." But she turned to Kate for a second opinion. When she did, I elbowed Byron and said, "It does look better on me, doesn't it?"

Byron just sighed, shook his bald head and rolled his big brown eyes.

When we settled into South Beach's Savoy Hotel —the only Ocean Drive hotel located directly on the sand of what's known as the American Riviera—I headed straight to the poolside gym and talked on my cell phone to my personal trainer-*cum*-boyfriend, Rick.

"I miss you babe," I cooed.

"Miss you too. Don't forget to think of me when you're squatting." That was his gentle reminder for me not to let slide the feel-the-burn exercise regimen he had designed just for me.

The warm and sun-kissed days passed as Byron and I watched our *TREND* ad campaign unfold: the very hip ad agency photographer took pictures of the *au courant* fashion photographer, once a judge on "America's Next Top Model," shooting glamorous *TREND* editors figuring out how they wanted the too-exquisite-to-be-real-people models (who seemed to always be eating) to pose.

There were also "before" pictures of the supermodels getting blowouts, comb-outs and makeup applied. Funny how their "before" shots looked a lot like most people's "after" shots.

It was always the same: Byron and I sat back on cushioned chaise lounges and watched through Oliver Peoples-shaded eyes at our "vision" coming to fruition.

All the while, I munched on carrots and drank plenty of water, and Byron ate carrot cake and drank fruit smoothies. All this tall, wiry man did was stuff his face and he never gained an ounce. "It's just my metabolism," he'd sniff. If he could bottle what he had, he'd put Slimfast out of business.

One day, as he was savoring a breakfast burrito courtesy of the craft services chef, Byron met my mystified glance and accused, "What? And don't tell me how many Weight Watchers POINTS it has; I really don't give a crap."

Well, I gave a crap and it was worth it, because on our off hours, I had the confidence to lay out by the luxurious pool surrounded by lush, tropical foliage with human mannequins whose bodies graced international magazine covers and were lusted after by men across the globe.

I always thought women like that would be vain and smug. But I was wrong. They may not look like the real women you ride the subway with everyday, but they were as real as any one of those straphangers. They spoke of men who wanted them, whom they, of course, had no interest in. Men whom they loved, but who didn't love them back, not for more than their faces and bodies, anyway. Fear of younger models who were still in high school; being cheated on; unappreciated. Their bouts of marriage-fever; baby-fever; and of course, the latest diets.

I also continued to work out in the hotel gym; sometimes the models were there too.

Once, we all left together and some young, clearly fashion-conscious teens were hovering outside the door, hoping their idols would sign some of their *Elle*s, *InStyle*s and *Allure*s.

"Are you a model, too?" one asked me. *She must think I'm one of those petite models.*

"Um, no, but I could be, don't you think?" and I struck what I thought was a modelesque pose.

She gave me one of those blank thirteen-year-old girl stares that said, "Grown-ups are such weirdos," and shrugged, before she backed away from me as though it were Halloween and she suspected I was doling out apples with razor blades buried inside.

Oh well, I couldn't be too offended; after all, she did say she thought I could have been a cover girl.

I was in heaven. The surroundings, the companionship, the chicness of it all. And on top of it, I fit in. This was the adult equivalent of sitting at the cool lunch table in high school.

If this was a business trip, may I do business forever.

One night, I answered the door to my well-appointed suite and it was Rick--surprise! What didn't surprise me was that he did something so sweet and romantic. He was such a gentle giant of a guy. I leaped into his arms and we headed right to the bedroom and stayed there practically all weekend. He even declined my invitation to be introduced to Heidi & Co. "What do I want to see them for? I have you."

Another night, after a hard day's work watching the bikini-clad models roll around in the surf, we all went out to a well-known celebrity haunt, Crobar, to dance off dinner. Everyone had eaten conservatively, except for the calendar girls, who had pigged out on purpose, it seemed, because they knew people were watching them.

"We do this all the time. People think we starve ourselves, so we shovel it in to freak them out," said Naomi with a wry smile.

We all laughed, but then I leaned over to Byron and whispered, "Should I show Carolyn Murphy my Weight Watchers book so she can see how many POINTS are in that deep-fried whatever thing she's eating?"

"Only if you want her to go get a restraining order," he answered, as though he were talking to a mental patient.

Being with a gaggle of supermodels really opened doors. When we got to the club, not only had the velvet rope been cast aside (hell, they threw it away) at the mere sight of them, but drinks were comped, and the riff-raff (who ordinarily I would be considered one of) were kept in abeyance.

After a couple of weeks, Byron and I said goodbye to Heidi, Gisele, Kate, Carolyn, Naomi, Tyra and Christie. We flew to Paris and followed around the editor-in-chief. There was unfortunately no time to sightsee. This didn't matter to me, since Paris is where I had spent my junior year of college. But, Byron, well, this was his first trip to Europe and I think he wanted glamour. Instead we got to run after this woman who had ignoring people down to a science. We fared better in Australia – dogging the photographer and travel writer around was sort of like being on a tour, the kind where the tour guides pretend you're not there. The vintage thing in L.A. had its moments. We shopped on Melrose and had dinner at The Ivy, where we watched Keanu Reeves try to look natural as he ate and talked to his companions, while the paparazzi across the street snapped away.

Then came the trip's *coup de grâce*. We were off to New Mexico to catch up with the journalist who was doing the Julia Roberts piece. Being a voyeur of the rich and beautiful was actually taking its toll. Not that I missed my 1-800-M-A-T-T-R-E-S or Greenwich Village nabe; I didn't even miss my newly decorated and semi-palatial office or my home away from home: the gym. I just got tired of sitting and watching other people work.

Byron and I both got a little annoyed as we stared down the ad agency photographer who was getting frustrated while taking candid shots of the journalist just sitting there and nodding at Julia as she answered his questions, ones she had answered only a million times before. "This is exciting," the photographer kept muttering as she rolled her eyes and snapped pictures with so little effort that I was tempted to grab the Nikon and start doing the shooting myself.

Byron said to the shutterbug, "It's supposed to be 'behind the scenes.' I don't care if he's doodling on her tablecloth and Julia's stirring her ice tea—shoot it." Then he turned his attention to me.

"So we'll be back in New York in a few days. What's going to happen with you and Lisa?"

Lisa Katz was another VP Account Supervisor at Image. We had gone from best friends at work to non-communicating colleagues soon after I slimmed down to goddess proportions.

"Where'd that come from?" I said. We had managed to avoid the "Lisa" subject the entire trip.

As Byron indicated to the photographer with a very intimidating and impatient finger, that she should take a picture of the reporter on the phone and Julia playing with her daughter Hazel, he said, "I've tried to stay out of this, but I talked to her this morning and she asked about you."

"Oh, really."

"I told her you were the same and that didn't sit too well," he said, implying that everything had been my fault.

He nudged me to walk him over to Julia's kitchen counter for a coffee.

"What does 'the same' mean?" I demanded to know.

"It means you're different. You lost weight and you became someone different and that hasn't changed."

"That's right..."

"I'm not talking about the way you look."

"Right again. I'm no longer that fat chick who wouldn't speak up in meetings because no one would listen anyway, since people don't like to listen to anyone they don't want to look at." I saw Julia look up. I guess I was being a little too loud.

I continued in a more dignified tone. "People like when you're down and out, and by out I mean..." I gestured with puffed cheeks and my arms curved at my sides to simulate a fat middle and hips, "...out-to-here. It makes them feel good. *Well, my life may not be perfect, but at least I'm not fat and self-conscious like her.*"

We walked over to a long table with proofs from the prior day and started looking through the pictures.

"Nobody is denying you your confidence. It's, well, I'll just say it. It's your arrogance that we could all do without."

"Arrogant is what jealous people call other people's high self-esteem," I said, before I tossed the proofs back on to the table and started to walk away.

"And by the way," I shouted back at him, "when I was out on the patio, Julia said she wished she had my legs."

# Chapter 1

## "Fat And Skinny Had A Race"

"C'mon, Trish. Craig wants everyone now," said Lisa, as she ran by. You would have thought the building was on fire the way everyone in the agency was scrambling. The daily ritual was to sit around the oh-so-hip and happening Soho shop (our CEO and President, Craig Silver was one of the first ad agency mavericks to move off Madison Avenue), doing our work (God help you if you were not working when he made his rounds) and waiting for the verbal alarm to go off: *Craig wants... Craig needs.... Craig says...*

Lisa was two years older than I was, having already reached the big 3-0. Unlike me, Lisa was married to an accountant, Joe, with an adorable two-year-old daughter, Lil.

I took her cue to get movin' down the black-carpeted hallway with the red and silver papered walls to the glass-enclosed conference room (Craig really missed Gordon Gekko's '80s when red, black and silver was the "it" color combination.) I hustled while I juggled a file, a pad, a pencil and chugged a chocolate Slimfast shake.

I don't know why I bothered starting the day being calorie-conscious. Every day was the same futile eating routine: Slimfast for breakfast. Salad bar for lunch. (Of course, so stressed by the time lunch rolled around, I always added stuff to the salad like croutons, tuna with mayo, breaded chicken cubes, sun-dried tomatoes, olives, peppers, artichokes. Am I leaving anything out?) I never seemed to leave anything out of the salad. Or on my plate. By mid-afternoon, I was so full of anxiety that I'd head down to the lobby for a Kit Kat, or two. If we worked late, which was almost always, on the dime of Image we had our choice of Chinese, Mexican, Italian... Well, let's just say that the U.N. commissary does not offer the array of ethnic delicacies spread out in our conference room.

"We work you, not starve you," chuckled Craig, who stayed trim forever on Atkins.

If neither of us had to put in O.T., I'd go to dinner with my boyfriend, Kevin. When I didn't see him, I spent my solo evenings with my other favorite guys, Ben & Jerry. (I don't like to cook just for one. B&J comes in the convenient pint size, single serving.)

The herd was now stampeding past me. If I were last to show my double chin in the conference room, I would be seen as lazy as well as fat. I took a deep breath and inhaled the last straw full of my diet *du jour*, then hoofed it.

"Lisa, wait up." But she had already entered. I hoped she'd saved me a seat so I wouldn't have to scramble for a chair; if I missed out, I'd have to stand for the whole meeting, which is a killer on little feet forced to hold up a big ass.

We were all assembled, and as usual we all ended up in a situation where we had to hurry up and wait. Craig was on his cell and obviously in no rush to get off the phone, even though about fifty people, with work to do, remained idle.

He stood up at the front of the room, gray at the temples, dark gray Armani suit, looking like the statue that was sure to be erected to this ad legend nicknamed "The Silver Fox." Rumor had it that Craig gave himself the nomenclature, but he swore it was bestowed upon him by *Adweek*, when they profiled him in the early '80s, and touted how every account he touched turned to gold.

Regardless of who gave him the name, the reputation was real. It all began in the mid-'70s when he was a college-educated mailroom guy at the now defunct Ted Bates Advertising. The agency was pitching the PanAm account. Craig, always privy to executive memos before the execs, read some data about the airline and figured out that the company had as many employees as seats on all of its planes put together; hence, technically there would be one PanAm employee for every passenger. This maverick mailroom guy ran to the office of the president of one of the world's largest ad agencies and pitched him the line: PanAm: One-to-One Service. He was promoted, not to Junior Copywriter, but to star Copywriter. Moments later, to Creative Supervisor. And about half an hour after that, to the position of youngest Creative Director in advertising history.

Five years into his skyrocketing career, he walked out of Bates with a fifty-million dollar piece of business and his own agency, hailed in the trades as the sneakiest and savviest move the industry had ever seen. He'd been going strong ever since.

The Fox was tall and slender; in pretty good shape for a sixty-ish ad slave, at the beck and call of demanding and, much of the time, unreasonable clients who could easily take ten years off your life every five minutes. He had manicured nails, a perennial tan, and a parade of designer wear, for business and dress-down days.

I've gotta say, Craig Silver knew his business. "It's all about image," he would remind us all time and time again; it made up for what he did not know about graciousness, sensitivity and diplomacy when dealing with employees.

He sent an account executive home once for showing up wearing a black Diane Von Furstenburg wrap dress the day of a major pitch. "You look like you're going to a funeral!" he screamed. When a senior art director and loyal employee asked if another A.D. could cover a shoot for him, because the guy wanted to attend his grandfather's funeral: "If your replacement fucks up, it's your ass," substituted for the customary yet ever predictable, "Sorry for your loss." And then there was that week when we had brought in several freelance computer graphics people to work 24/7 to help us pull a major client presentation together. The night before the meeting, when all was finally said and done, and the finished product could only be described as stellar, Craig poked his head in to "politely" ask the freelancers to "clock out," as he was not going to pay them for sitting around, eating pizza and saying their good-byes.

No one ever called him on his take-no-prisoners deportment, because, well, he was the supreme ruler there, and everyone was scared of him. One word from him to a headhunter or honcho colleague and you'd never write a jingle in this town again.

When I interviewed at Image over five years ago and tipped the scales at what a boxing trainer would categorize as a "light weight," I thought he was the most superficial man I'd ever met – even for the advertising industry. He kept looking me up and down, gazing at my dewy twenty-three-year-old face and slender shapely form, while mentioning how he could definitely put me in front of the client. I really wanted to tell him to shove the account job, in fear that he would start pimping me out to get business, but I knew that an assistant account executive position there, as opposed to the giant agency I was getting lost in, would put me on the top of the ad heap. "You work at Image? For Silver?" people would ask with an awe reserved for archangels who report directly to Jesus.

I got used to the cachet of working for the cool guy in the hot place. So to secure my status, I busted my ass. Obviously the quality of my account work secured my place there, because he didn't let me go after I no longer fit the image of Image. I had become one of those people whom others describe condescendingly as having "a pretty face."

Right after I took the job, my fiancé, whose name I shall never repeat again until the day I die when my last request to God will be to send him to hell, dumped me for one of those MAWs (model, actress, whatever).

We had met in senior year of college. Allow me to qualify. My spiky 'do-ed dude had not gone to college. He did not even finish high school. Landscaping was his day job, and we met when he yelled at me to "Get the fuck off the grass, coed bitch." His charms increased when he noticed my CBGB's t-shirt and apologized immediately. "Sorry. Sorry. You're obviously cool. I'm just in a bad mood."

He was so cute and cool and unlike anyone I knew, that I forgave and forgot to go to classes the rest of the afternoon. I offered him half of my oversized peppers and eggs sandwich compliments of my mom. I had not gone away to school, but lived at home, and as in high school, commuted down from Westchester to the Bronx. That afternoon on the campus of Fordham University, we talked about his musician hopes and dreams until he knocked off work around five.

We started dating, which entailed listening to songs he'd penned, following him to open mike nights, and comforting him when yet another band member would bite the dust, or a paying gig would turn out to be some pre-teen's birthday party.

This made his rationale for leaving me all the more unfathomable.

He claimed the MAW was more devoted to his music career than I. I, who carried equipment into rock clubs so seedy I feared for my life to go solo to the bathroom. I, who insisted that I knew in my heart that every trite piece of crap song that he wrote was on a par with anything Lennon and McCartney ever churned out. And I, who swore I would support him with my meager entry level ad gal wages because I knew I would get it all back (with interest) when my tattooed millionaire's first album went platinum – any day.

The real reason he dumped me: my rival's dad was the head of A&R for Geffen.

I had stayed thin for that man. Forget thin. I was anorexic for him, mostly because I didn't want to lose him to some smoky-eyed, heroin-chic groupie. The ones who wear a lacy, black Victoria's Secret bra as their shirt. I lived on diet Coke and salad with lo-cal dressing. I popped Correctol to flush myself clean two or three times a week. I was boney, yet I looked in the mirror and thought I looked attractive. Seeing my hip bones protruding was an accomplishment. And where did it get me?

Since I needed a paycheck and could not stay in bed with the covers over my head forever, I ate my way back from rejection depression and became what my Rocker used to call the "fat chick," who only looked good at 4 a.m. through beer goggles. "The bigger the cushion, the better the push in," his band used to joke.

Craig said nothing about my altered appearance. He also did nothing, like put me in front of the client, but I knew he liked my work because he hadn't fired me.

Finally off the phone, the Silver Fox started rapping on the top of the black marble table that commanded the middle of the 30x40 foot room, and the buzz from its inhabitants came to a dead silence.

"OK, now why did I call this meeting?" Craig joked, tapping his tanned and wrinkle-free Botoxed-temple with his manicured index finger.

The group groaned in that good-natured, "Oh boss, please don't tease us," way.

"Oh goody. Shecky Silver is going to do *schtick*," whispered Lisa. "I feel like I'm twelve and back in the Catskills suffering through dinner and a show with my parents."

"He reminds me of my uncle, who'd get drunk at wakes then get up and 'say a few words' about the deceased, as though the funeral home was his big shot on Leno," I added.

Lisa was Jewish and originally from Montclair, New Jersey. I am Irish Catholic and hail from Riverdale, the Upper East Side of my borough. It worked for us. Sort of a same-sex Stiller and Meara. Although so many people thought we had gravitated to each other because we were both Irish. Black Irish that is. Fair skin with dark features, like Colin Farrell or Jennifer Connelly. "I'm Jewish!" Lisa used to make clear when someone would ask if she knew how to make corn beef and cabbage. Finally, she got her husband to buy her a huge gold Star of David for her birthday so "They'll see my Jew-ness coming a mile away."

"OK, OK," Craig said like a snarky emcee, who knows that the crowd would rather hear the band than his banter, but he's going to make the crowd wait just a little bit longer to "build up the excitement." We all knew we were there to hear the big changes that were happening at our ever-growing and glowing agency.

"I'll get right to it. This has been a banner quarter for us. Three new clients in two months. The departure of some of the agency's higher ups. Voids need to be filled, so here goes. For the Hanes Underwear account, stepping in as the new VP Account Supervisor will be Lisa Katz."

Applause, applause, deafening applause. I was so proud of my pal. I gave her a friendly nudge with my elbow to encourage her out of her modest little wave/ mouthed "thank you," combo and into a Broadway-esque bow from the waist, but she wouldn't. "Show off" was never her style.

"And...settle down people," demanded our master of ceremonies, "and the *TREND* Magazine account will be headed up by new VP Creative Director, Byron Jackson."

Thunderous applause. I caught his eye and gave my guy friend the thumbs up. No one deserved *TREND* more than dapper, gay, and creative genius-y Byron from Jackson Heights, Queens, who had totally transformed himself from street kid to chic kid so he could get into the Manhattan scene. His diction had become so impeccable, that he was often asked if he was British. He always answered, "Yes." Then under his breath he'd snicker, "Me and Madonna."

"And the new VP Account Supervisor will be, of course...," continued "Shecky" Silver. He started looking around the room with his index finger pointing to the crowd and twirling in a circle. He had this, "where is that person," look on his face.

"I'm here, I'm here," I wanted to spring up and say. I knew it wasn't going to be me. But a girl can dream. I had grown, literally, into the image of someone that Image could no longer put in front of the client, even though I had put in all the long nights, the research, and written the account brief and presentation that had helped bring in the business. Technically, I was part of a team, if you can call working with Chelsea the Barbie doll a teammate.

She had not even wanted to be an account executive. To anyone who would listen, she told the story, with pride no less, of how she had taken off between her junior and senior years of some third-rate upstate community college, moved to New York and started waitressing between catalogue modeling gigs.

When lo and behold, one day she waited on The Silver Fox. Next thing you know, he convinces the restaurant's manager to let Chelsea take her break so she could join him for a bite. He told her that if she was going to step, fetch, and wait on people, she should do it with more prestige.

Well, her looks had worked on her behalf once again. She used to tell people that she had been "a geek," a total ugly duckling in high school. She had heard supermodels tell that tale on *E! True Hollywood Story*, and in other interviews done for the *Style Network*. Chelsea liked how it sounded: modest, as though the whole beautiful-face-staring-back-from-the-mirror thing was all new.

Truth be told, Chelsea had had the body of a Hooters waitress and face of a cover girl since she was thirteen and knew how to use it.

After lunch, Chelsea quit her job and was escorted by Craig back to the agency for the grand tour. The next day she started as an assistant account executive. She still did, and still does, catalogue modeling. She is the image of Image, even without a B.A., since she has the BS down pat.

Well, the only thing she did as part of the *TREND* new business pitch was present to the client, because Craig called it her *forte*. I did everything else, *aka* the legwork.

"I don't care," I convinced myself. "Being a workhorse beats being a show dog any day," I kept telling Kevin. "Boo-YAH!" he would say, then we'd fist bump in a mock reenactment of him and his Wall Street buddies.

I was about to jump out of my skin. Craig's finger was twirling, twirling, twirling. Round and round it goes, where it stops I don't know as long as it didn't point to...

"Chelsea Tyson," said Craig. That bleached blonde bitch was going to be my boss. Lisa put a supportive hand on mine, then I clenched my quivering other hand on top of hers; until we both had to break free for the obligatory applause. I looked at Byron who mouthed the words, "You're still on the team." I smiled and applauded like the trained seals I used to see at The Bronx Zoo.

Lisa leaned in reassuringly, "Byron's saying you're on the team."

"Yeah, second string," I said.

Chelsea, looking like a Score's pole dancer stuffed into a tasteful, yet flirty, Banana Republic outfit, did that palm-front-then-back hand wave favored by doll-like beauty pageant winners on parade floats or bored members of the Royal Family.

To my ears, the applause from her adoring fans sounded like machine gun fire.

# Chapter 2

## "What's Eating You?"

There's just nothing like a good chomp on a milky brown Hershey's Bar to chase the blues away. Some people live to eat. Others eat to live. I eat to deal, so I can go on living. I learned this at an early age when food, more specifically dessert, even more specifically "a nice piece of cake," was held up as the cure-all for whatever ailed me.

I missed honor roll by a point? I'd get a nice cup of tea and a scone slathered in butter. Tripped during the ballet recital? Nothing soothes a bruised ego like an English Muffin pizza created by me and supervised by my mother, who by the way never partook in said treat.

By the time I reached twelfth grade, I could lick my wounds (from opposite sex crushes gone awry to girlfriend cattiness) by licking ice cream, scarfing salty Lays straight out of the large yellow bag or downing Oreos after drowning them in giant glasses of whole milk.

I always felt so much better, until the problem that had been "eating" at me went away and I would be left with a big "fat" reminder of it. Then I'd always feel so much worse than I had about the original issue that plagued me in the first place. *Then* I'd go on a diet. I'd feel so much better, until the next "crisis" that I had to eat my way through. Then...

I had been doing this for over a decade. I shrugged it off as, "just the way I am," and remained the creature of my bad nutritional habits.

So there I sat, alone in my middle-management, two-window office that overlooked my favorite Manhattan view – Starbucks, McDonald's, Subway, and our local greasy spoon. Without guilt or shame, I unwrapped an Almond Joy, because sometimes you feel like a nut. Of course, at that moment, mid-unwrap, was when Byron chose to poke his smooth, shaven, chocolate head in. I suddenly craved a Milk Dud.

"You OK?" asked my newly promoted pal.

"Nothing a truck load of Kisses won't cure." I had bitten off such a hunk of "Joy" and was chewing multiple almonds, that even without a mirror, I knew the chocolate, combined with my saliva, had coated my usual pearly whites with a slimy russet glaze. I didn't care how unattractive I looked.

"How could they do this? I helped bring in the business. What did she do?" I didn't care how I sounded either. I was talking with my mouth full, so it came out like, "Ha coo ey oo is? I elped bing in a binuss. Ut id see oo?"

"Well, my little chocoholic, she's got a track record too."

I had swallowed by then. Hard.

"But not on this...I..."

"Look, Miss Trish. Byron will not BS. The account is *TREND* Magazine. She looks like she could be in *TREND*."

"...but I..."

"I know, but...dear God, will you put down that candy bar, girl. I'm gettin' diabetes just lookin' at y'all." When Byron got riled, his King's English took the 7-train back to Queens.

I looked in disgust at my sugary salve that had melted all over my fingertips, made a mental note to buy M&Ms next time, and threw the candy in the trash.

My phone rang. Byron used this saved-by-the-bell moment to excuse himself so he could stop watching my now brown-laced lips get smacked by my brown-lacquered tongue. Well at least they matched.

"Hello. Trish Collins," I sighed into the phone.

"Hey Doll Face. It's me."

Kevin's voice was crackling, so I knew he was on his cell.

"Hey you."

"Hold a sec so I can give the coffee-cart guy my money." I rolled my eyes as I listened to rustling and polite banter. Kevin never liked service people to think he was "too good" to stop and chat. It was part of his self-consciousness about growing up with servants.

Yes, not only had roly-poly me found a decent man in New York City, but a wealthy one at that, as well as handsome and just plain nice. Even more unbelievable, was the way we met.

It was a little over two years ago at a Noho bar called Decades – dark, dingy, loud and incredibly happening. They had four rooms, each embodying days gone by. One recreated the psychedelic '60s; another the disco '70s; next was the glam '80s, and finally the grungy '90s. My three slimmer friends were off being hit on. Two of the girls, work people whose names I don't even remember, went off to the '60s for free love and freer drinks courtesy of their "dates." My new best friend at work, Lisa, headed to the '80s with a non-'80s guy named Joe, so they could mock the we-wish-greed-was-still-good crowd.

I sat by my lonesome at the '70s bar, not looking for Mr. Goodbar and pretending, "That's the way, uh-huh uh-huh I like it." Sitting catty corner from me were two girls, clearly, to me anyway, high schoolers made up to look like what they envisioned twenty-seven to be. I was about to turn twenty-six and even I got carded. *Was the dude working the door asleep when they hobbled in wearing their mommy-let-us-play dress-up stilettos?* I watched as two guys approached.

One, tall, dark and smarmy, introduced himself as Robert and gave the full court press to the mini-Kate Moss of the pair. Her black cigarette jeans and black baby-T on the real Kate probably would have looked incredibly cool. Mini-Moss looked, I'm sorry, cheap. She giggled and batted her Sephora-globbed eyes the way she must have imagined that sophisticated "older" women (you know, like twenty-two), did it.

The clean-cut, All-American guy with Robert, seemed hesitant about hooking up with Kate's friend. His stance and demeanor screamed wingman.

Wing shuffled his feet, kept his hands tucked deep into the pockets of his navy Brooks Brothers trousers, and seemed to strain to make conversation with the other young woman. She had a Cindy Crawford mole, but that was the only thing "Cindy C." about her. She too wore skinny jeans, but in denim. Her black t-shirt announced "Hottie" in red rhinestones. Aside from tacky, she also looked vapid. It was hard to believe that her interests could possibly reach any farther than getting used to wearing her class ring.

When there was a pause in their dialogue, he looked around the room, presumably for an escape route, and our eyes met. I pointed out his choice of companionship with my chin, and made a face like, "You're kidding, right?" He sighed, gave a momentary glance up to the disco-balled heavens, then raised his eyebrows like, "Help."

So I got up off my zebra-printed stool, walked over from behind his teen angel, and in my most dramatic turn to date, pointed and declared, "There you are." Then with hands on hips à *la* Alice Kramden, I continued with, "I left the baby at home alone again so I could come out and track you down." I then looked at the girl, who had obviously never seen such a confrontation, except perhaps on *Melrose Place* reruns, and lectured, "Men. You can't live with 'em. You can't shoot 'em. Or wait, maybe I can," as I dug deep into my geometric-patterned Le Sport Sac shoulder bag. Thinking I must be going for my Saturday Night Special (*sans* permit), teen Barbie slid off the stool and bolted for who knows where – perhaps the '90s, since that was the decade in which she was born.

When "the father of my child" was able to control his gut-holding laughter, he managed an, "I'm

Kevin Gallagher and I owe you – big," and proceeded to get the attention of the bartender who was dressed like John Travolta in *Saturday Night Fever*.

Kevin was 5'10, with sandy brown hair. He was trim, not because he worked out, but because like so many young on-the-rise New York men, he ate a hearty corporate lunch with clients each afternoon, then didn't have time to eat dinner because he got too embroiled in the late night assignment he was working on. During the course of our fun and flirtatious conversation, he said modestly that he was a Philadelphia Gallagher, which meant absolutely nothing to Bronx girl me.

He had gone to Harvard undergrad, then The Wharton School of Business for his MBA, which naturally got him recruited by Goldman Sachs as an investment banker, like his father and grandfather and great grandfather and...

"I've kind of had my career planned out for me since I was two. Some people, by people I mean women, like the dollar signs they see above my head but, find me a little too, um..."

Boring?

"...unadventurous," he conceded.

Not me. I had already had enough adventure for one lifetime, being the "ex" of a future Rock God with a groupie back stage at every venue and a heroin habit waiting to be rehabbed. Steady. Stable. Secure. Predictable. These buzzwords were the new music to my ears. I longed to hear the request, "Let's not go out tonight."

"I hate clubs like this," he confessed, "but I come because if I stayed home everyone would know how truly dull I really am."

"I'm a social retard myself." I neglected to mention that I used to live in clubs far worse than this. "I'd rather stay home and watch TV or a DVD…"

"…with a bucket of Newman's Own popcorn…," Kevin added.

"…with my own addition of melted butter laced with garlic."

"Is there any other way?" he winked.

Kevin Gallagher was a nice, solid, boring guy and even had the Eagle Scout troop leader face to prove it. Jackpot!

After a few drinks and far more laughs, I said I had to go. As much as I wanted to go home with Kevin, I was not quite ready to expose my watch-it-wiggle-see-it-jiggle full-bodied self to someone I didn't want to scare away. I let him walk me outside to get a cab, but he insisted upon seeing me home, then up to my apartment. Had I actually found a gentleman in New York City or the next Ted Bundy?

At my door, he asked, "Did anyone ever tell you that you have a face like a porcelain doll?"

*Well, maybe he could come in. I'll get undressed in the dark. I know! I'll pretend I'm kinky and tie his wrists to the bed. This way he won't be able to grab a handful of flab.*

Then he kissed the apple of my cheek with his warm, slightly chapped lips and added, "I really enjoyed your company. I'll call you."

*How original.*

But he did.

Kevin seemed to like me the way I was, and grew to appreciate me, especially my blue-collar background work ethic. I knew he would understand why this Chelsea promotion thing was so wrong and unfair.

"OK, I'm back. So what happened at your big meet..."

"Trish got dissed," I sighed.

"Get outta town. You helped bring in the damn account."

"Kevin...Don't remind me."

I could hear him huffing and puffing. "Where are you?"

"Across the street from work. I'm running. I'm heading back from my 8:30. I've got to get back for an eleven o'clock meeting. I stopped for a caffeine refuel, so I've got to hustle. There was too much traffic to even think about sitting in a cab."

I loved my little hustler.

"So, listen, Doll Face, I'm sorry."

"You know who got promoted?" I asked as I watched an encore of Chelsea being congratulated by all, only this time the venue was the agency's hallway. "Chelsea."

"Oh," he mumbled.

"Yeah, oh."

"Well...you know, I can kind of understand."

He could what?

"What do you mean you can understand?" I said as I bolted up out of my ergonomic black leather desk chair like a rocket just given the go-ahead for blast-off by mission control.

What followed was the sound of backpedaling on the other end of the line.

"No...I mean you deserved it, but...it's *TREND* Magazine. I guess they wanted someone to work on it who looks like...um..."

I began having a hallucination: As Chelsea was walking down the hallway, I envisioned, for a split second, that it had become a Bryant Park Olympus Fashion Week runway upon which she was cat-walking, complete with a rock music sound track, photographers' flashbulbs popping and plenty of twirls and poses.

As my awake nightmare turned back into the agency's hallway, I finished Kevin's sentence. "She could be in *TREND*."

"Yeah, like that, you know."

"Yeah. I know."

"Look, tomorrow night we'll work on your resume and ..." Then I heard him say, but not to me, "Hold the elevator."

"What about tonight?" I whined. Seeing him would keep this day from being a total loss.

"I can't, Doll Face, I gotta go to this work thing. Rubber chicken, the works."

I plopped back down into my chair. Guess I'll be seeing Ben & Jerry for dinner then. I knew we had to wrap up because he was back in his office building, but... "How come I never get to go? Other people are always going to stuff at their boyfriends' jobs," I baby talked.

"This isn't that kind of thing. I gotta go."

"But it's Friday night," I tsked like a petulant teenager who'd been grounded.

"I know, but...I gotta go. You'll think of something to do."

I already had. I'd spend the evening trekking down Rocky Road.

I lived in the West Village in my grandmother's former apartment. Think Monica on *Friends*, except without the second bedroom or terrace or skylight or fireplace or... Bohemia was really not for me, but the place was rent controlled, and even though I was there illegally, until the "law" came a lookin' for me, it was my home. I dreamed of the Upper East Side, so I Ethan Allen-ed Grandma's place, so that, at least on the inside, it looked as though I resided in a one-bed in the East '80s around Lexington.

I sat in my boring, beige terrycloth robe opened to reveal a gray T-shirt and matching underpants, a consolation gift compliments of Lisa and her new access to all things Hanes. To complete the ensemble, I was wearing the ever-stylish white sweat socks which helped keep my Origin's creamed feet from staining the sofa cushion's fabric. One dimpled leg stretched straight out, slightly bent at the knee, and the other rested comfortably over the back of the blue-striped couch. As I scooped up the ice cream out of the burgundy, black, green and white carton and into my mouth, by the blue glow of my 32" boob tube, I listened intently to the affected commentator of *E! Fashion File*: "...the slacks ride low on the hips to show off the season's other fashion essential: the bare waist accessorized with the thinnest chain link belt."

I sought comfort from my most stalwart supporters, "Not if you're a Chunky Monkey. Right, Ben? What do you think Jerry?"

## Chapter 3

### “Eat and Run”

The next morning, I left the famed New York rat race for the summer, suburban scenery of leafy Westchester, where my sixty-year-old mother now lived.

We had relocated in my sophomore year of high school, after my father died. His death was not a prolonged misery caused by illness that we accepted before it even happened. It was swift and unexpected, and took us completely off guard.

While crossing Riverdale Avenue, one of the main thoroughfares of the Bronx, he was mowed down by a hit-and-run driver. It was a Sunday morning, and he had gone to the bakery to get us cinnamon buns as a special breakfast “for my girls.” When he hit the ground, the bag burst and the buns were strewn all around him. The pedestrians who ran to his rescue had to shoo away the pigeons that thought they had been invited to an all-you-can-eat buffet. Taking into consideration all the garbage I have consumed over the years, nothing with cinnamon as an ingredient has ever passed my lips. The mere smell of it makes me sick.

Even though I was able to continue in my same high school, I was still taken away from everything I knew. I couldn’t walk home with the girls; I had to catch the train. I couldn’t run home and change and meet everyone to hang out in Van Cortland Park; I had to catch that train. And if I wanted to go to a dance on

Friday nights, I had to sleep at someone's house because my mother refused to let me come home alone at midnight on, you guessed it, the train.

Suddenly my life revolved around times of day like 6:59 a.m. and 3:42 p.m., and especially Monday through Friday's 5:54 p.m., when my mother's train from Manhattan, where she worked at the phone company, pulled into the station.

It was around the big and emotional move when my first real bout of yo-yo dieting began. My mother and I were both sad, but being a teen, I had the added joy of being sulky and weepy as well. My mother, who had always been happy and smiling, had now become very pragmatic. "He's gone, but we're still here. We have to move on." She was also very unselfish, making my feelings her priority. We'd sit down for dinner and she would let me jabber on and on (I was never quite sure if she was ever really listening) over dessert, a "nice" piece of pound cake *á la mode* she'd customized just for me. They were works of art, her desserts: whipped cream, sprinkles, a Marischino cherry on top. Yes, there's nothing like a fruit that smells like red Magic Marker to say, "I love you."

She, of course, had only a cup of tea. If I polished off the cake and ice cream before our talk was over, she'd give me another dollop of whipped cream. I started junior year in a brand new uniform skirt and blazer because I had gone up two entire sizes over the summer. My mother asked me if I had been snacking when she wasn't looking. How could she not notice that I was eating all the food that she put in front of me?

Metro-North was as packed with people as an issue of *TREND* is packed with ad pages. I ended up having to stand while I drank my strawberry Slimfast shake and read the *New York Post*. A sleeping forty-something man, showing signs of gray at the temples, was jarred awake when we reached 125$^{th}$ Street and realized that by taking up two seats with his belongings, he had deprived many of us a comfortable ride through most of Manhattan. I believed for a moment that he was a gentleman, when he moved them aside for me.

"Forgive me," he said. "Here, please sit down. I'm so sorry. So, so sorry."

OK, already. You didn't kill anybody's mother. "Thanks."

He kept staring at me with still half-asleep eyes and hooded eyelids, as he sort of smiled. I guess he noticed that I was getting creeped out, so he reassured me he was harmless by announcing, "My wife is pregnant, too. I know all about swollen ankles."

*You couldn't have stayed in dreamland, right, fella*?

Too embarrassed to admit to my fellow passengers, who were now staring, that, "No, I'm not with child. I'm just the proverbial fat chick," I stifled a primitive scream, turned up the corner of one side of my mouth as if to imply, "Thank you for moving your junk," and returned to the gossip and canoodling that is *Page Six*.

I was able to walk from the train depot to my mother's house. She lived on a cul-de-sac that was open and welcoming. Neighbors waved and kids on bikes had room to ride or choose to play basketball without leaving their mother's sight. A far cry from the way I grew up on our crowded, yet lively Bronx street, where the stickball game was interrupted every two minutes by a car.

I headed up the steps of my mother's modest two-bedroom brick with small family friendly backyard, got the mail from the black box that hung next to the front screen door, and entered using my own key.

"Mom, I'm here. Where are you?"

"In here, Patricia," she singsonged.

"Here" was the sunny kitchen made sunnier by its yellow curtains and accessories. I walked through the burgundy, floral print living room and Country French dining room into the breakfast nook.

My petite and thin mother and equally fat-free Aunt Emma were sitting at the canary Formica table. I am my mother's only child and my aunt's as well, since she never had any children.

"Mmmm, what smells good?" I had to know, because as my dad used to say, "this woman can cook!"

My Irish father had married an Italian girl. My olive-skinned, dark-haired mother was a traditional creative genius. She could not only cook, but sew, garden, and decorate. She was Martha Stewart before Martha knew she was Martha Stewart. I inherited nothing from my mother except for her diminutive size. I have my dad's coloring and his face. That's probably why my mother was always staring at me, searching for a glimpse of her lost love.

"Brunch," my mother answered with reticence.

"Sorry I missed it. Any left?"

*Well, I'd done it. Asked the dreaded question.*

My mother and aunt glanced at each other. The only thing worse than having a mother, who disapproves of you, is having two.

"There's some on the stove," answered Mother, in a tone that stated clearly, "If you want it you'll have to get it yourself. I will not contribute to making you fatter than you already are."

"I'll just have a little taste," I lied.

I scooped myself a hearty helping of fluffy scrambled eggs she'd seasoned with onions, peppers and oregano, took a few strips of bacon which had been fried on a low flame to absolute crispy perfection, and a slice of French toast made with thinly sliced Italian bread.

When I joined them at the round table, Mother and Aunt Em looked disappointed at my full plate. It made me feel disappointed in myself. So... I drowned my sorrow, as well as the French toast, in maple syrup.

"So how's work?" my aunt wanted to know just to change the subject away from my dietary indiscretion. Or just to get me talking so that I couldn't put anything in my mouth.

"Not too good. I didn't get the promotion I wanted." Just the thought of Chelsea in "my" office with "my" title and "my" bump in pay made me drizzle on even more Mrs. Butterworth.

"Did they say why?" inquired my mom. Her annoyed tone was now directed at the horrible people who had denied something to her brilliant and capable daughter.

"No, they didn't have to say. I know. It's *TREND* Magazine, so they gave it to this model-type."

"*TREND*? Oh, I guess they only want to work with people who look like they could be in the magazine."

What was that? The standard comment for when you don't get a job with a fashion magazine? Is it in some fashion reject handbook somewhere or something? That remark sent the seasoned eggs shoveling in.

"Didn't you eat breakfast, lovey?" asked Aunt Em, who happened to look at the wall clock in order to take her eyes off my unnerving and uninterrupted fork-to-mouth hand motion.

"No. Well. Yes. Well, I had a Slimfast earlier."

"Are you on a diet?" Mother wanted to know, half excited, half confused.

"Always, sort of."

"Then why are you eating that?" She said, "that" as though it were something vile I had dug out of the garbage instead of food she had prepared.

"You'll never work with *TREND* if you eat two breakfasts," chimed in my aunt.

"Guess not."

Shovel. Shovel.

"You'll get sick. It's not good to feel so full," added my mother for the full effect of the double nag.

I dropped the fork defiantly on my empty, except for a strip of bacon, plate.

"Guess so."

"We're only saying it for your own good," defended my aunt.

"Don't you want to look nice? Does Kevin ever say anything about your weight?" interrogated my mother.

"No. I guess he figures I get enough insults from my family."

"Who's insulting you?" said my mother in all sincerity. Aunt Em backed up her sister with, "Yes, who?"

My aunt just had to know, "You don't eat like that when you're out with him do you?"

"When we go out to dinner, we don't keep tabs on each other's food intake." I was running out of steam for comebacks.

My mother couldn't resist, "Don't get mad. We just want you to look nice. They probably picked that other girl, because she can wear all the nice style clothes, right?"

"I have nice clothes," I said through gritted teeth.

"Oh, nothing looks nice in those big sizes. They never lay right over bulges."

My aunt nodded in silent agreement like some sycophant subordinate. As my mother started to clear the table, she went for my plate first.

Before it was out of reach, I swiped the last piece of Oscar Meyer and bit down on it hard. In their faces to spite them both.

## Chapter 4

### "Pulling Your Weight"

"Pass the grapes," I requested of Byron at our Monday morning internal *TREND* strategy meeting.

I munched and munched on grapes from the fruit platter, pretending they were green M&Ms, while Chelsea, looking even more glamorous than usual, sashayed around the room like a pin-up girl; her steel gray Armani suit jacket, just like the boss was wearing, was off revealing a sleeveless, slate blue, v-neck silk blouse. She used her Pilates-toned arms to gesture at rather typical print ads the client had already run, and her Marilyn Monroe-ish voice, to pontificate about where they ran (as if we all hadn't seen the Times Square billboard), and who shot them (even though it was common knowledge that *TREND* used only famed photographer, Giles Bensimon), and which models were used (because no one in the room recognized Carolyn Murphy, Christy Turlington or Elle McPherson).

Just watching her strut with such confidence, the kind that comes from looking good and knowing that people are enthralled with you even if what you're saying is pedantic, or dare I even say, inaccurate, was enough incentive for me to not grab for the melt-in-your-mouth chocolate chip muffin I had been eyeing. I refused to take it, not so much because eating one would make me look and feel fatter, but because watching me eat it would make Chelsea feel even thinner and more self-assured.

I monitored The Silver Fox seated at the head of the table in his black leather swivel chair, the only one in the room with arms, as he became transfixed by Chelsea. Like all men, you could just tell, he liked keeping his eyes glued as she moved. I had to admit, regrettably, she was a great presenter. But like even the best Oscar-winning actresses, she may have been able to say the words with aplomb, but still didn't, or couldn't, write the script to save her life.

Before her promotion to VP Supervisor, when she was just an Account Executive as I still was, she had her assistant AE write her marketing briefs and presentations. Now that she was bumped up, she'd be having me do them. Honestly, not to be mean, but half the time, I really didn't think she had any clue what she was talking about. Apparently that didn't matter as long as she could sound convincing.

"Ok," said Craig. "This is what they've done in the past. I personally am not impressed, but did the ads do their job? Did they talk to the market and persuade people to subscribe?"

Oops. A question that needed a knowledgeable, marketing response. One that a "supervisor" should be able to answer right off the top of her bleached-blonde-with-black-roots head. Chelsea started plowing through papers in her overstuffed disorganized folder.

"Um. The market...um...liked...um...didn't really respond to... uh..."

I rolled my eyes, got up out of my chair, reached across the table, for what I was sure everyone thought would be a glazed doughnut with rainbow sprinkles, but instead pulled out the bright yellow fact sheet from her file with data regarding previous advertising stats.

"This one has that information," I announced.

I was about to read it when Craig snatched it out of my hand and handed it to her. I guessed that if he had to look at someone spewing off boring statistics he wanted it to be someone worth looking at. She started reciting as though she herself had done the research.

You're welcome, bitch.

At this point, Byron was pretending to take notes with one hand and shading his eyes with the other, so that he didn't have to witness me being humiliated.

"As I was saying," announced Chelsea. "The market responded..."

You could tell Craig was thinking, "All this and brains, too."

I was thinking, "Someone comfort me." So I reached past the fruit and grabbed the closest muffin, which was more than happy to feed my poor soul and face. Ah, blueberry to chase the blues away.

I then pushed my chair back away from the conference table so I could eat in peace, and also because clearly, I would not be missed.

# Chapter 5

## "Super-size Me"

"...and then he asked her a question that, of course, she didn't know the answer to because she knows nothing except how to accessorize and get her boobs to pop out of her suit jacket, and I hand her the friggin' paper without even an acknowledgement that I was assisting the team... then he takes it out of...."

I, in what-a-day mode, had been chattering away while Kevin and I shared a piece of Black Forest German chocolate cake that sat on a plate which had been sprinkled with powdered sugar. We always ate out, usually in his Upper East Side 'hood in one of the seven-thousand restaurants or cafés that lined Second Avenue, and catered to the young and up-and-coming. Even though I didn't blend in with the many thin blonde prep-school-looking women whom this area attracted, I still felt more comfortable than I did downtown where I was surrounded by people with blue hair, black leather and multiple piercings. I thought Kevin was listening attentively, until, as I came up for air, I caught him checking out an attractive, red-headed waitress.

I wondered how often he did that.

I stopped talking, pulled the cake plate closer to me, then stabbed the luxurious brown mass for an extra big forkful.

The next day, I met my mother for lunch at Saks Fifth Avenue in midtown, since she did not have the where-with-all to schlep to Soho. Our meal was the usual cavalcade of questions about when I was going to lose weight so "I would look nice," a never-ending series of gestures to other women whom she deemed to "look nice," and extra large helpings of food being pushed in my mouth to keep me from telling my mother how much I hated her.

When I had had my fill of both my Caesar salad and my mother, I volunteered to walk her to Grand Central where she could catch Metro-North and I could then hop on the #6 train back downtown. I did this, of course, to make sure she got there safely, and to guarantee that she was off the island of Manhattan and far from me.

We exited the store on Fifth, and as we turned the corner, there in one of the 48th Street windows was the most beautiful cocktail dress I had ever seen. Simple. Black. Halter. And fitted at the bottom. Rows of sequins at the hem made it divine. I was having a sweet daydream right there in the middle of the side street. Oblivious to the crowds and chaos of lunch hour Manhattan, I saw myself in the dress, twirling on Kevin's arm on a penthouse balcony under the New York City sky, spotlighted by the illumination atop the Empire State Building.

As Kevin kissed me sweetly, the music in my head screeched to a halt and was replaced by my mother's nasal, "Forget it. You've got to have some shape to fit into that, kiddo."

Talk about a buzz kill. Her words were like a needle that scrapes across a record, tearing up a beautiful melody and diminishing it into an unbearable scratching.

With tears in my eyes, I turned away from the window and my mother.

Lo and behold, a hot pretzel vendor to ease my pain. "Could I have that really salty one, please?"

Back at my desk, I decided to make up for my doughy treat by designating Slimfast to replace a Snickers as my mid-afternoon pick-me-up. While I sipped, I looked up and saw Chelsea in the hallway flaunting some new designer outfit and toting the July issue of *TREND* as though it were a clutch bag.

Just as I was having second thoughts about that Snickers...

"Trish Collins," I sighed into the phone.

"Hey, Doll Face, you OK?"

"Swell." I actually was a little better for hearing Kevin's voice.

"Right, listen. Bob called."

"Oh, Christ," popped into my head and fell out of my mouth in a whisper. I was in no mood to hear evoked the name of Bob the Modelizer. From the first night I met Kevin when I saw Bob sidle up and introduce himself as Robert to that prepubescent, "outta boroughs" Barbie, I hated him. I got it in my head that Kevin was only there as his wingman to be polite. After we started dating, I could not believe that Kev really thought of that greasy playboy ad sales rep and former college roommate as, "my brother from another mother."

"What?" said Kevin.

"Nothing. He's just..."

"Yeah, well," he said to not let me get started on his buddy. He knew how I felt and obviously didn't want to hear it...again. "Anyway, he's got a new girlfriend and he wants me, you know, us, to meet her. He says she's the one."

"The one what? The one who's even stupider than the last one?"

Kevin couldn't help but laugh, "I don't think that's possible."

"Let me guess. She's an aspiring model and actress. Is she at least out of school? I really don't want to hear another story of how some teenager is going to send her high school graduation picture to modeling agencies."

"No. This one's already a model. A real one. Bessie something. He says she's in magazines and stuff. She's famous."

How this man could be a financial genius, yet so gullible at the same time is beyond me.

"Famous, huh?"

Kevin wanted to know if I'd ever heard of her.

"Heidi. Yes. Gisele. Yes. Bessie? Uh, no," I admitted with a little too much pleasure in pointing out how full of shit his friend was. So, it was my turn to back peddle. "But maybe she's a newcomer to the realm of supermodels and just hasn't crossed my path yet. So where are we going?"

"Bungalow 8."

"Bungalow 8? As in *Page Six* Bungalow 8. Where Diddy has his birthday parties and Paris dances on the tables? How are we ever gonna get in to...?"

"She's a model. Those people can get into those places. Listen, I told Bob you might not want to go with us, so don't feel obliga..."

He'd go anyway? I see that a hot club – or is it the models who patronize it – is all it takes to draw a homebody off his Lazy-Boy.

"No, I want to go," I assured him.

"OK then, I'll be by at nine. Later."

"Later," I said to an already dead phone line.

"Byron?" I whispered conspiratorially.

"Yes, Miss Trish," he said without looking up at me from his stacks of fashion magazines. When he finally did, he sighed and continued with, "You've got chocolate on the corners of your mouth."

"It's Slimfast," I said in my own defense.

"It's still chocolate," he countered.

I wiped and said, "Cover for me with Chelsea. Say I'm in the bathroom if she's looking for me."

"I do not know what you are up to girl, but you know, she is your boss. I think it's time you decided to grow up, accept and respect." Then he snapped his fingers in the air at me.

I told the Bessie-Bungalow 8, need something to wear, story and he sighed with a head shake and hand wave, "Go. Just don't take forever. Unlike me, she can go in the ladies room to look for you, remember?"

The cab driver got an extra generous tip for defying all laws of traffic and gravity to get me uptown to Saks "fast" as I had instructed in the most restrained scream I could manage.

Once inside the store, I frantically went in search of the dream dress from the 48th Street window.

"May I help you?" asked the ultra-sophisticated saleswoman, who, about twenty years ago, could have posed for the pages of *TREND*.

I huffed and puffed, "There's this dress in the window. Black...v-neck...gathered here... sequins down here... and..."

"This dress?"

As if by magic, she had made appear my fantasy frock. I could have kissed her, but something told me that that was not done on the designer floor of Saks Fifth Avenue. "Yes, yes, that's it."

She gave me a pity smile and conceded, "It's beautiful and really flatters a, shall we say, a certain figure."

I guess I looked as though I was ready, willing and able to wrestle it away from her if I had to, so to avoid a scene...

"Let's see, you'd be a size..."

I barked out a number in hopes it would reach the sensitive ears of the benevolent fashion gods who would miraculously let that become my size.

"Right. Sometimes, in a garment such as this the next size up might work better. Here. This is the largest it comes in."

How I managed to zip this dress up the side, I will never know; perhaps a sheer act of will and the goddess of cocktail dresses smiling down on me.

I was short and squat with two chins, but who's counting. My thighs were always in danger of being chafed when they rubbed together, so I always had to either wear pants or pantyhose. I refused to shop at Lane Bryant no matter how nice the styles in the window looked. I always bought the largest size in a "regular" store. That was why everything I owned, no matter how cool or chic, looked like, what's the technical term for it? Oh yes. Sausage-casing. I was constantly tugging.

I stood there looking at myself in the mirror really hard, as though I could have willed myself thin by burning off the fat with an intense gaze and imagined laser vision.

I ignored the bulges that were conspicuous to say the least and chose not to notice how the zipper pulled on each side so that the material that was supposed to flap over it was so stretched out you could see the threads holding the seams together. "If I don't walk, or sit, or move, I think I can get away with this," I pep-talked myself aloud.

"Excuse me?" asked the hyper-efficient saleswoman who thought I was speaking to her through the door. "May I come in?" And she did before I had granted permission.

"How are we?" she asked graciously.

"We're thinking about it."

She swung the door wide.

"Let's have a good look." And she did. A long, hard, disapproving, good look. *I already have a mother, thanks.* The look was just long enough for her to figure out how to tell me in a nice, I-still-want-to-make-a-commission-off-you way that the dress did not fit. "You know, we don't have this particular style any larger, but I might be able to find something just... almost like it... perhaps similar in Misses."

"No," I barked in a tone I had not used since I was in high school and started sassing my mother. "I... I mean, no thank you. This'll be fine. I plan on wearing higher heels," I informed her as though from a higher altitude the fat would evaporate.

She realized that she was fighting a losing battle. And what did she care? She'd make her percentage on the dollar. So, with a patronizing smile, she acquiesced, "Heels can make all the difference," then asked, "Cash or charge?"

The trip back downtown to Image would have qualified my cab driver to compete in the Indy 500.

I snuck into my office unnoticed, like a teen who'd broken curfew, not believing that I had gotten away with a mid-day shop. Chelsea was nowhere to be found, but Lisa was hot on my heels.

"Wha'dja buy?"

"Shhh," I screamed in a whisper. "A dress. Kevin wants me to go out with his idiot friend Bob and his girlfriend 'the model,' to Bungalow 8."

I dropped my shopping bag and purse as though they weighed two tons.

"Wow, maybe I'll read about you tomorrow on *Page Six* of the *Post*."

"Kevin likes for us to stay home most nights and just be together, but I guess because it's this hot place, he wants to go. I don't mind...it sounds, cool, you know?"

Before hanging up my suit jacket, I emptied my pockets, but first I waved the receipt around.

"I bought a three hundred and fifty dollar dress that I can squeeze into if I don't breathe."

I then tossed the Juicy Fruit on my desk.

"I also bought twelve packs of gum to chew so I don't eat anything between now and...," I turned sideways and sucked in my gut, "...when I have to put the dress back on."

For dramatic effect, I filled my cheeks with air, "...because one false move with a saltine and I'll explode."

Lisa was a few beats of the conversation back. "A model, huh?"

"Yes. Bessie the model," I shrugged, still clueless as to who she was.

"So is she a real model or one of those 'aspiring' ones?"

"Kev says she's in magazines. I don't know."

"Bessie? Bessie... You, know...I think.. Wait a minute."

Lisa ran out and I tried to get settled in case Chelsea came by. I didn't want to give her the satisfaction of knowing that I had slacked – even momentarily.

Lisa came back in with the latest issue of *TREND*, which she had pinched from Byron, and opened it to a page with an ad for L'Eggs Queen Size Panty-Hose. Yes, even fat girls read *TREND*, with the dream that someday they would lose the flab and become *TREND*-worthy, which was the client's catch phrase.

Lisa slapped the publication down on the desk in front of me and said, "Bessie."

"Bessie?"

"The plus-size model," added Lisa.

I started to laugh. Nervous, uncontrollable laughter. The big, boisterous, body-jiggling laugh of a fat chick.

"So Bessie," I choked, "the model," I weezed, "is... is... is... Bessie The Cow model," I screamed over my own hysteria.

Lisa had a bout of contagious laughter, but managed to keep her humanity.

"Stop it. You know she's got her own talk show on cable. I've seen it. She actually comes off really nice. She's pretty," Lisa said adamantly.

"Yeah, she's got a 'pretty face' like all us fat girls."

# Chapter 6

## "Weigh Your Words"

That evening, no longer intimidated by the thought of hanging with a human hanger, I enjoyed getting ready for my glamorous night on the town at a notoriously, cool club with my handsome, young, successful boyfriend. Beat that, Chelsea. She, of course, was always out and about, and rumored to have plenty of men. She was even pictured in *Vanity Fair* once on the arm of some ballplayer at a charity gala. But still, she had no one special as I did.

In front of the bathroom mirror, I put on more make-up than usual using *TREND*'s how-to-get-this-look diagram.

With different pages of hairstyles cut out and taped to the wall, I fussed with my ebony mane, which had grown past my shoulder blades because I had not had time to go for a trim. When I couldn't quite get the knack of the French Twist, I gave up and let it cascade about my shoulders *á la* a '40s movie star.

When I went into the bedroom to get dressed, my exercise bike, with clothing hanging all over it, reminded me how invaluable this piece of fitness equipment had always been. It was like extra closet space; another place to "hang my hat."

I didn't put on a bra so that I could eliminate an extra layer of material (and bondage) between me and "the dress" in the hopes that I was giving myself room to breathe.

On the way home I had stopped and purchased a pair of Spanx, high-priced super-all-over-control pantyhose, which sucked in and smoothed out my bumps and bulges quite efficiently.

There, that was one topic Bessie and I could talk about: L'Eggs vs. Spanx. Compare and contrast. Each team has five minutes. I looked like a *Cirque du Soleil* performer as I took a really deep breath, contorted my body forward to make my stomach as concave as possible, then proceeded to wriggle and writhe until I had stuffed myself into the coveted cocktail dress.

The drama ended with a flourish as I used the hood of a wire hanger to grip the tab of the zipper, shut my eyes and yanked it up in one deliberate motion. When my eyes opened, one at a time, and I did not see any rips or tears, I exhaled, then inhaled again immediately realizing that holding my breath and stomach in were the only ways I would possibly be able to survive my fashion choice.

Still adhering to the philosophy that my shoes would be the key to helping me slim down, I squished my feet into my three-inch black heels, then waddled into the foyer and looked in the mirror as I added my grandmother's antique marcasite earrings and matching bracelet. Just as the finishing touches were on, the doorbell rang.

I opened the door slowly then stood there so Kevin could take in the glamorous, painstakingly put together me.

He barreled in missing me completely, without even a kiss or hello.

"You ready or what? Let's go," he said with anxiety I had never before seen him display.

Still trying for my "A-ha moment," I sort of pitty-patted around in my dress, awaiting a compliment.

I got tired of waiting, and watching him pace like a caged tiger.

"Well?" I asked in exasperation.

"What?" he said without a clue.

"My dress."

"Oh. Yeah, it's nice. Kinda tight, but, that's OK...it'll be dark. Doll Face, c'mon we're late."

I pushed past him, grabbed my black, albeit dated, Pashmina, and slammed shut the light switch.

"What? I said you looked nice," he said in that confused, What'd I do now? guy way.

I left him to shrug and close the front door behind us.

We pulled up in a yellow cab not quite in front of Bungalow 8, because the limos were triple-parked. Since I was seated on the curbside, Kevin had to climb over me to get out first so that he could first get a grip on both my calves as to turn me sideways facing him. Then he helped me slide to the edge of the leather seat. With the toes of my shoes bumped up against the toes of his wingtips for leverage, he took both my hands and lifted me out of the taxi.

Because there were some celebrities headed into the club, all eyes were not on Kev or me, so I was able to quickly regain my dignity. I took yet another deep breath and we walked toward the entrance where we found Bob the Modelizer and Bessie Plus-Model, awaiting our arrival.

"Kev, Trish, this is Bessie," said Bob. "Bessie, my pal, Kevin and his girlfriend, Trish."

When did Bob, looking considerably less oily than usual, acquire such genuine manners? Whenever I heard him be polite before, he always sounded like Eddie Haskell from "Leave It To Beaver."

"Hi, heard a lot about you," said Kevin as he shook her hand in a very professional, everyone's-a-perspective-client way.

Sort of hiding behind Kevin, I said, "Hi," with hands remaining at my sides. I was afraid that if I used too much energy talking or lifting my arm to shake hands that my dress would burst open. I was positive Bessie probably took me for snotty or just unsophisticated, but she was gracious just the same.

"It's lovely to meet you both. Robert has told me so much about you, as well. We can talk more inside. Shall we?"

With that, an extremely poised and cordial Bessie led the way in. Bessie truly was a Plus model. She was strikingly beautiful, plus statuesque, plus flawless makeup that accentuated her cornflower blue eyes, plus a formfitting, strapless pale blue knee-length dress that fit her to a T, plus a great shoulder-length haircut with shimmering blonde highlights, plus perfect posture.

All eyes followed her. Where had I seen such confidence before? Oh right, my colleague-*cum*-boss, Chelsea.

Bob followed Bessie, Kevin went after him and grabbed my hand to pull me along. A self-conscious me took up the rear – literally and figuratively – all the while using my Pashmina to cover myself up.

Like the Red Sea, the velvet rope parted for Bessie and the bouncer gave her a kiss that signaled she was one of the regulars.

Bob turned to Kevin, who nodded in approval.

I couldn't help but think, "Since when do fat chicks get this kind of respect and attention?"

Once inside, Bessie worked the room. Her warmth and self-assurance made her a people magnet.

Because of her, we were all invited to sit at a banquette of "beautiful" people – no actual celebrities, but more behind-the-scenes celebs: agents, editors, stylists, and those of independent wealth whose job it was to just travel the world and hang with famous friends. Everyone was talking and laughing, drinking and enjoying themselves, except for me.

The whole scene had the high-school-nerd-at-the-popular-lunch-table component. And the dream dress wasn't helping matters any. The outfit I had romanticized, the one that, once on, would make it all OK, had failed me. I felt so uncomfortable. It was hard to sit and breathe at the same time. I felt bad because I thought everyone was noticing that I looked as miserable as I was. I felt worse when I realized that no one was really noticing me at all.

At the head of the table, Bessie and this guy, who was either also a model or played one on TV, began to argue playfully, in French no less.

Everyone enjoyed the show, clinking their glasses, applauding, shouting things like: "Touché" and "Bravo."

Kevin leaned into me and whispered, "Bob's actually done it this time. No wonder he said she's the one. Bessie's really impressive, isn't she?"

I shrugged and sniffed, "I never thought I'd see the day when I'd get shown up by someone more than fifty pounds heavier than me."

He looked disappointed that I was being so bitchy and argued, "Granted, she's a big girl, but she really pays attention to her appearance not to mention she has confidence out the ying-yang." He elbowed me as he pointed out, "Maybe she could give you some tips."

Tips?

"I didn't realize you thought I needed tips," which I said a little too loudly.

Kevin smiled an embarrassed there's-no-problem-here smile at those who noticed my outburst. Then to me, backpedaled with, "No, I mean..." Pedal, pedal, pedal, "It's just that you're so pretty, maybe she could..."

There was steam filtering from my nose. I felt like a teakettle.

"Never mind, forget I said anything," he sighed, then turned his attention back to the table.

Just then, for the drama of it all, I decided it was time to get up in a huff and excuse myself to the ladies room. My intent was to emulate Bette Davis as I had seen her in many a Turner Classic Movie. I would twirl my cape then exit stage left.

Up. Huff. Twirl. Rip.

I stood staring into in the bathroom's mirror, estimating the damage: a still zipped zipper torn at the seams, lost beads, loose threads. Well, I thought, at least now I could breathe. I felt tears welling up in my heavily black mascaraed eyes, shame crawling up my spine, so stiff and achy from sitting straight so I could hold in my stomach, disgust at my stupidity and vanity working its way up from my scrunched toes and taking over my entire body.

And in breezed Bessie.

"I'm sorry we're not sitting closer to one another. Robert tells me you work on the *TREND* account. We need to get together so we can dish about the industry. Great night, huh?"

I nodded to my split seam that I was pinching together with my fingers as though that would some how mend it. "Well, not for all of us."

"Oh, no," sympathized Bessie. Did she have to add "plus so nice" to her seemingly endless list of attractive qualities?

She dug into her compact, yet chock-full, handbag and pulled out what looked like half a gross of safety pins and some Hollywood Fashion Tape, which she referred to as "miraculous."

Glad to step in for the assist, "Here. Allow me." Bessie worked her model magic, first with the tape, then the pins for added support. She was not only beautiful and kind, she also smelled good. Since we were so close we could have been wearing the same stilettos, I couldn't help breathing her in and wanting more.

"I'm sorry. I just...I have to ask. What fragrance is that?"

"Oh," she gushed as she pinned like a professional seamstress. "It's my own. I've just closed a deal with Coty. We start marketing it in the fall."

"It's lovely," not sure if I meant the perfume or its creator. Up close, I could see past the makeup to her genuine sweetness and optimism. She really was lovely.

"It's called "Breathtaking." A little flowery; a little fruity; very light and fun." And then she was done with me. "There."

"Were you a seamstress in another life?" I said trying to be witty.

"No," she answered as she admired her handiwork, "just proficient in the tricks of the trade."

"I need to lose a little weight," I said shamefully stating the obvious.

"Or just buy the next size," said Bessie, also stating the obvious.

"The next size, well..., the dress didn't come in it, and even if it had, I'd cut the fat off with a knife before I'd be caught dead wearing a size..."

Oh, yes, my mouth is also big and fat.

The I'm-a-helpful-person smile disappeared from Bessie's porcelain-like face and made one last minor adjustment to my dress in a perfunctory I'm-a-bigger-person-than-you-are-both-literally-and-figuratively way.

"There. That should hold you."

"I'm sorry, I didn't mean...I mean, you're probably a size... but you look..."

"...great. I look great, " said Bessie as she admired herself in the mirror and completed my awkward run-on sentence.

Then she turned squarely to me, looked me straight in the eye and said, "You know, there isn't a thin girl inside me crying to get out. This is me and I believe in making the most of what you've got. And I like what I see. If you can't say that about yourself, then do something about it. Or you'll spend the rest of your life coming apart at the seams. And that can't be fixed with tape and pins."

Bessie exited the ladies room with composure and pride, leaving me alone with my makeshift self. I did not like what I saw in the mirror.

## Chapter 7

### "May Cause Shrinkage"

The dog days were upon us. Unless you were sunbathing on Central Park's Great Lawn or at the promenade by the East River, or overlooking the Hudson by Chelsea Piers, summer in New York City could be an oppressively nasty place. I was sweating off pounds and inches just standing on the fry-your-egg-here sidewalk as I watched the pink neon "Weight Watchers" sign sizzle in the second floor window of the five-story building on 7th Avenue South.

To give myself an excuse to keep walking, I reminisced about the first time I had embarked on a diet-plan drama-rama, as opposed to previous attempts to lose weight when I just skipped meals or just didn't eat.

It was the beginning of junior year in high school. I went to a school lovingly referred to as Snob Hill. Although it was indeed located on a hill, the snob part was riding upon the coattails of a reputation from long ago and far away, when the school opened in the 1930s and only wealthy families could or would send their girls to a private learning institution. The only girls attending the all-girl school now, were plain old middle-class Bronxites like me. If anyone actually thought they were better than anyone else, like her father was a fireman instead of a sanitation worker or bartender as mine was, then she was truly a legend in her own mind.

As it had been the case for a couple of years, my friends and I were sick and tired of the Bronx. Because I knew my mother was meeting my aunt and a friend for dinner, thereby unenslaving me from the Metro-North train schedule, I convinced my crew to go right from school to 8th Street in Greenwich Village and buy that year's fashion must-have: Ol of Daughters clogs.

We didn't know our way around the Village, so we didn't find the shoe store, which, as it turned out, was around the corner from the subway station, until we had wandered around for two hours and our feet were too swollen to properly try on the shoes. The best thing that happened that afternoon was that I meandered into one of those tourist traps that sell t-shirts, posters and anything that will fit the letters N.Y.C. on it.

There on the rack of cards that spouted headlines such as, "Greetings from New York Fucking City" and "New York Women are the best!" over a picture of transvestites, I spotted a postcard that would change my life. It was a black and white photo of a very young girl kneeling by her bedside praying. A little Catholic girl just like me. The caption, in bright yellow, read: "Thank you God for my pretty face, but this fat ass has to go."

There was one left. I convinced myself that in all of the universe, only one existed, and it had been created just for me. I gave the cashier a buck, folded the talisman, and put it in my wallet where it would stay while I embarked on my self-created weight-loss plan: tea for breakfast, soup for lunch, and whatever my mother made for dinner.

It took me six months, but I wore a junior size-five gown, a demure little navy spaghetti-strap number with a white floral print and white bolero jacket procured at Lerner's on Fordham Road, to Tommy Kelly's senior prom.

The next day, back on 7th Avenue South across from Weight Watchers, it was even hotter, so I watched the neon pink sign sizzle from inside the Dunkin' Donuts. I contemplated how right Bessie had been about changing my appearance, as I was dunkin' my honey-glazed treat in my cup o' Joe.

The following day, I watched from inside the neighboring Pizza Hut. *Whoever thought of baking the mozzarella into the crust is a culinary genius,* I thought, as I mulled over how very much I wanted to lose weight.

The day after that, I had every intention of watching the pink sign from the refuge of McDonald's, as I washed down my Big Mac with, for comic relief, a diet Coke; however, when the woman on line ahead of me, with so many rolls of fat that she looked like a Shar-Pei, ordered what I was going to have, I decided, "Let's just get this over with."

I exited the elevator and approached the non-fat, but also non-intimidating looking counselor at the long mahogany reception desk.

"Welcome to Weight Watchers. Would you like to register today?" My way of saying yes was to slide the clipboard off the desk and take a deep breath as I began to fill it out.

The Weight Watchers trim and friendly group leader, who was once a two-hundred pound member, addressed the meeting room of mostly women and a few men. I sat way in the back like a remedial student who shows up for attendance credit, with no plans to participate. I wasn't one of "them" – yet.

The meeting leader said, "Weight Watchers is devoted to a comprehensive approach to weight management…"

As she spoke, I dug through the pockets of my oversized denim shirt and found a melty, but edible orange Starburst.

She continued, "…through an education program directed at lifestyle change in an atmosphere of group support."

I got up and took off my shoes, joined the line and waited my turn for me, my blue cotton button-down and navy sweat pants to be weighed. This outfit was so inappropriate for the weather, I was surprised that I had not passed out. But I'd rather have roasted than reveal my cellulite to the world, or at least to the bustling bohemia that is downtown Manhattan.

I grew alarmed as those around me started stripping down to sports bras and bike shorts before stepping onto the scale. Was this the exhibitionist Weight Watchers location?

The group leader still kept talking. "First, we assist in determining a weight goal that is appropriate for you."

I could still hear her words, two months later, as I shopped for weekly groceries, hurrying past the white, black and orange-wrapped Halloween treats display at Food Emporium, and making a beeline for the Weight Watchers frozen breakfasts, snacks and dinners. She was saying, "The Program is built on sound scientific principles in the areas of nutrition, behavior and exercise."

My airy, pre-war one-bedroom apartment was short on closet space, but I found a way to make room for my clothes in the closets I did have, then dusted off my low-tech, yet still usable, stationary bike.

The pounds started to come off, slow and steady. I never told anyone what I was doing. Not Kevin, not Lisa, not my mother, nobody. I wanted this to work, and I knew from experience that once I told people I was on a diet, it would become my M.O.

"How's your diet?" "How much have you lost?" "Oh c'mon, it's so-and-so's birthday. One piece of cake won't kill you." For as long as I could remember, there had always been diet demons and detractors out there. I would not be sidelined. I would rather lie and say, "Cake. Not with this stomach ache," then say I was watching my weight. I also did not want every pound shed to be the topic of other people's conversations. "*Did you see Trish*?" "*Yeah, she lost two more pounds*." "*Really, I thought it was more*." "*Actually, I thought it was less. She's still kind of chubby*."

I also vowed not to get new clothes until I had reached my goal, so I hid in my old ones.

Kevin and I shared Thanksgiving dinner with my mother and extended family. As the peas covered in cheddar cheese, sweet potatoes, as well as mashed, and stuffing were passed around the crowded table, I took only a small dollop of some, and of others, none at all.

Everyone was too busy talking to notice my portions; always my erstwhile Weight Watchers group leader's words reminding me, "Every food is given a POINTS value based on its calorie, fat, and fiber content. You'll choose your meals to stay within a Daily POINTS Range."

I noticed changes in myself, as well as my body. I now ate my low-fat ice cream from a dish, as opposed to the waxy carton.

People of course, started to notice: my single chin; the lack of bloat in my face; the absence of chocolate in the corner crevices of my mouth. Still, I did not reveal myself. "I had a little flu thing; I haven't really been eating," I'd say. As a chemist knows the symbols for the periodic table, I had learned the POINTS equivalent of most foods, so I no longer had to sneak to peek at my POINTS counter booklet every five minutes.

As luck would have it, Kevin had been traveling a lot on business, and even when he was around, he was totally consumed by some big multi-zillion dollar deal he was working on. "I can't pay attention right now, Doll Face, my 'Berry's blowin' up." Sex had not been a big priority for us, so even if he had been around, he probably would not have seen me naked anyway, but I was glad he was absent while I was working on becoming "less of a person."

He gave me a beautiful David Yurman silver bracelet accented with peridot gemstones before he left for Philadelphia to spend Christmas with his family. He apologized profusely for not being around to ring in the New Year with me. His mother wanted the Gallagher clan to spend the holidays skiing in Aspen. "She just wants the family. I'm so sorry I can't invite you, but you know how it is."

Actually, I didn't. My mother was and my father had been very inclusive people. If they knew your name, you were invited. If they'd seen you around, you were invited. If you knew someone they knew – have a seat.

But not all families are the same, so I said I understood. It was just as well. Some New Year's Eve Bash with booze flowing and cheese cubes in abundance could have created a major diet setback. I would have a quiet night with Ryan Seacrest counting down from Times Square and stay on track.

At my mother's New Year's Day get-together, where I wore a big, bulky ski sweater and leggings, no one even paid attention to the fact that I took a piece of cake, then cut it in half and fed the other half to the cat.

In January, Kevin was off again on some deal his firm was putting together and I was free to run the last leg of my weight loss marathon without risk of exposure.

By the time Spring had sprung, even before I showed up for my weigh-in, I knew I had arrived. The Saturday morning that I stepped on the scale, garbed in

Nike sports bra and bike shorts, (hey, when in Rome) as expected, I had reached my goal. The other members supported my hard-earned victory with sincere cheers and applause.

As I had heard our group leader say many times, "If the Program is the heart of Weight Watchers, then the support you receive in the meetings is its soul."

She also said that, "Celebrating your successes are a vital part of long-term weight management."

On the Saturday before Easter, when Kevin headed to Philadelphia to visit his family, I had the whole warm and sunny day to gather most of my fat clothes and bag them for my extremely generous Salvation Army donation. I kept some things that were fashionable and planned on getting them altered. But all in all, I needed all new things, so I split my time and money between only two stores: Banana Republic and Ann Taylor. I realized now, the entire world of exquisite New York City stores was my oyster, but baby steps, as they say, baby steps.

I got off the elevator on Image's floor and everyone was scurrying about as usual. "*Craig wants... Craig needs... Craig says...*"

As I walked down the corridor, head held high, in my new fitted suit, with a new highlighted 'do and Lancome's spring line on my face as the whipped cream and cherry on top, the whole place came to a deafening halt.

I then finally understood the phrase, "The Sound of Silence."

"Good morning," I chirped to dumbstruck colleagues as I passed, but no one greeted me back. They just stood, frozen, with their mouths open.

I entered my office and the almost scary sound of nothing was interrupted with a strident, "Who the hell are you and what have you done with my friend?"

I smirked at a bright-eyed Lisa and rolled my eyes as I responded, "Very funny."

"Seriously, what...?" said Lisa, seeming so genuinely happy to see me looking better than she ever had since she'd known me.

"Weight Watchers," I confessed. "I promised myself when I reached my goal, I'd get a makeover at Bloomingdale's and clothes that actually fit me."

"How could you not...?"

"I didn't tell anyone, not even Kevin. I just thought I'd have more of a chance the less I talked about it."

Just then Craig burst in. After all, it's his agency. He doesn't have to knock or say "excuse me," even though people were engaged in conversation.

"Trish, the client decided to show up and wants to see the media...what happened to you?" He then actually realized that that was too incredibly rude even for him and stammered, "I mean, you look..."

"Here's the proposed media plan. Tell Chelsea when she presents it to make sure to mention..."

"Why don't you present it?" said The Silver Fox, who stood in my doorway transfixed, staring at me like I was the last pork chop on the plate.

"It is your work after all," he continued as his gaze dropped down my torso then up again, leisurely.

"Well, Craig, I'm flattered, but I really don't know the client, so..."

"Well, then it's time to change that. You are on the team." He stepped aside to allow me to exit the office in the pretense that he was a gentleman, but I believe the gesture was meant as a way for him to eyeball my behind or lack thereof. I was dying to exchange amazed looks with Lisa and giggle, but I had to remember we weren't twelve-year-olds.

I had called my mother the night before and asked her to meet me for lunch. She was waiting for me in front of Saks.

I saw her notice me coming out of the cab. She did a double-take.

"My God, what happened to you?"

"Good to see you too, Mother."

When we got into the department store's eighth floor restaurant, The Café, she was still staring at me as though I were a stranger who had hypnotized her into lunching together. She snapped out of her trance so she could nag.

"And you didn't let me help you?"

Had we not lived in the same house? Had we not lived one life? I sighed the "take a deep breath" sigh needed by someone who must explain something that should already be known.

"Remember in high school, every time I went on a diet? That would be the day you'd bring home Entenmann's chocolate cake?"

"Well, just because one person is on a diet, that means no one else can have a piece of cake?" Welcome to my mother's logic.

"I just didn't want to be sabotaged."

"Who would sabotage you?"

"Fine, I just wanted to do it on my own without discussion. Can we order, please?" Then I snapped open my menu.

"OK," she said, as she counter-snapped hers. "But what can you eat?"

"Mmmm, I'll have the side order of baked ziti as my entrée...that's about five POINTS...and a side salad...with lo-cal dressing is about two."

"Ziti? What kind of diet lets you have all that cheese and carbohydrates?"

And she wondered why I didn't want to talk to her about my weight loss plan? I ignored her and turned my attention to the young handsome waiter/actor/model who was obviously taken with me.

That evening, I instructed Kevin to bring over a movie, *9 1/2 Weeks*. I said I'd make a little something for dinner.

I answered the door in a red silk, with white lace trim Victoria's Secret teddy, something I never thought I'd own, let alone wear. Needless to say, we skipped dinner. Later, Kev and I snuggled under the covers as we watched the movie. During the scene where, in front of an open refrigerator, a blindfolded Kim Basinger is being fed lots of different foods by Mickey Rourke, Kevin said, "This is the sexiest scene in the movie."

"Yeah," I agreed, but felt the need to mention, "it's impossible for her to keep track of all the POINTS she's eating."

Kevin laughed and gave me a hug that led to more interesting shows of affection. I believe that evening was the first time in our years together, we actually put "Mickey and Kim" to shame.

A couple of weeks later, we walked from my West Village neighborhood to the East Village and wandered into Ricky's drugstore, famous for its quirky combination of the basics and the erotic. Kevin wandered behind the beaded curtain into the Erotica section.

He looked like a fish out of water, a baby-faced frat boy searching for items with which to play a prank on a new pledge. I was shocked when he came out with something, unashamedly and not exactly whispering.

"Look, chocolate body syrup."

"Let me see," as I examined the label. "See this. Look at the fat grams...this is a million POINTS. I can just tell."

I walked away, and he followed me, still holding the bottle, like a kid who was not leaving the supermarket without the Bosco, no matter what his mother said.

"How about if I just eat it off you? Please? Trish? OK?"

When we got home, I prepared my dish of ice cream for TV time.

He followed me to the sofa and before our butts hit the cushions, whoa…

I hoped chocolate body syrup would come out of the cotton-blend fabric. I made a mental note to buy Shout stain remover.

Later that night, I woke up feeling a little sticky from that body stuff. I didn't think I'd be able to fall back to sleep, so I gingerly slid out of bed, so I wouldn't wake Kevin. Just as I was reaching the edge of my mattress, his beautiful, soft hand reached out and pulled me back to make love again.

"Right on the couch?" asked Lisa.

We were the first to arrive in the conference room and sat with our heads together like a pair of teens in study hall, while one by one, our colleagues made their way in.

I lowered my voice as I continued my soft porn story. "I barely had a chance to put down my ice cream. Then, later, in bed..."

"Again?" said Lisa, whose voice only got louder.

"Sorry to interrupt," interrupted one of my mild-mannered co-workers. "I just want you to know, you look amazing. It's like you lost half a person."

"Right, thanks." I think that was a compliment.

"Anyway," I continued to Lisa, "we've had more sex in the last two weeks than we've had in the past two years."

Interruption number two, this time from a sassy assistant: “Girl, I heard about this transformation...you lost a ton o’ weight.”

“Yes, well, not exactly a ‘ton’ but, um, thank you.”

Back to Lisa, “It’s...I don’t know...I can’t describe, it’s...like...

“Great,” she says. “That’s the word. It’s great when your man wants to have sex with you every five minutes.”

“And tonight, he can finally take me to one of those work parties he’s always got to go to, and he told me to go buy something new...on him.”

Just then Byron joined in and we gladly turned our *tête-à-tête* into a *tête-à-trois*. “Trish the Dish – that outfit is delish.” Snap snap snap.

Suddenly I realized that everyone was in little clusters and they were all looking at and talking about me. Some were giving me the thumbs up; others the “OK” sign. I should have felt like a movie star being spotted by the paparazzi, but instead I felt like a freak show creature: *The Incredibly Shrunken Woman.*

Then – drum roll please – Chelsea stormed in like a woman ready to find her man in bed with another woman. “Aha! – I heard I’d find you here like this.” She looked me up and down with squinty eyes and pursed lips, turned on her heels and took a seat on the other side of the room with her back to me.

I had never been so flattered that someone was giving me a dirty look and making a disrespectful gesture.

Chelsea was actually threatened by me now. I was real, legitimate competition. Although she had always known that the full-figured me could best her blindfolded in the back room crunching numbers, she had me when it came to going in front of the client to pitch or present. She had the confidence of someone who knew she'd win every time because physically, me and my pretty face could not measure up. She knew I wouldn't even try to compete. I had made it so easy for her to always be the center of attention.

But now, I could beat her in the back and front of the room.

Lisa leaned in and observed, "Do you realize in the last five minutes you've gotten more compliments than I've gotten in my entire life?"

"You know, I knew that I needed to lose weight, but from the way everyone is acting, I must have been a bigger tub than even I thought."

The Silver Fox came in and the meeting commenced. When it was the *TREND* account team's turn to present an update to him, Chelsea, as senior member, rightly did the honors.

"...and women eighteen to thirty-five make up...um...oh, I had those figures a minute ago...they make up..."

To save her ass, as usual, I pulled copies of the necessary papers from my folder. I started to pass the sheet up to her. "Here you go," I said in the straining-to-remain-professional way to which I'd grown accustomed.

As the paper made its way up to Chelsea, Craig intercepted it, and this time handed it back directing me to present it myself.

Chelsea's nostrils flared, making her look less Victoria's Secret Angel, and more Tasmanian Devil.

From my seat, I said, "Well, women eighteen to thirty-five..."

Craig then gestured for me to move to the front of the room alongside Chelsea. Standing next to her was something I actually avoided before. Now as an "after," I stood shoulder-to-shoulder with her, wanting to apologize for making her look bad.

I smiled to myself as I saw Byron and Lisa smile at each other.

# Chapter 8

## "Eat Your Heart Out"

Kevin, in my favorite navy, pinstriped, Brooks Brothers suit of his, which brings out the sapphire specks in his grayish eyes, proudly escorted me in my clingy, Cynthia Rowley silk, chartreuse, strapless, tea-length dress, on board the 120-foot yacht his department had chartered for its annual booze cruise.

The boat was packed, but in a the-more-the-merrier way. It was like Kevin couldn't wait to show me off to the older and distinguished partners as well as his young, bullish co-workers. He didn't even wait until we happened to run into people. He led me right over to them and one by one made introductions proudly.

"So nice to finally meet you," said a plain, yet pretty, colleague in a basic black spaghetti-strap dress, punctuating the word "finally" with a smirk.

"Yes, finally," emphasized another woman; again, plain, but this one not so pretty and in basic black. Hers was a sheath. Even though they were "dressed," they still looked all business, not to mention angry, the kind of anger that comes from being let into the boy's club, but never actually being treated like one of the boys.

I guess that's why their bitchiness was directed at Kevin, not me. He ignored their tones, already had made eye contact with someone across the deck, and began to lead me away.

Kevin had a very dignified way about him that I admired. Having grown up in Philly society, he stayed silent and composed when people were rude or antagonistic, smiled an "I'm better than you" smile, and excused himself. I, having had my social skills mastered on various Bronx playgrounds and schoolyards, was always ready to call someone out and throw down when they started with me.

"Um, yes, well, nice to... um, finally meet you as well," I had to practically shout back to the two women who had abruptly turned their attention to a partner passing by them.

We made our way over to his work buddies, who looked oddly just like Kevin. I made a mental note to keep Kev close so that I would not lose him in this sea of blue Brooks Brothers and Thomas Pink.

"So you do exist," chuckled an already inebriated Buddy One.

"We were beginning to think you were his imaginary friend," said an even snarkier Buddy Two.

The third buddy clinked my glass with his. "Here's to your health."

The three amigos burst out into what I think they thought was contained laughter, but what was actually rude, sophomoric snickering. These are the actions of men who make high six figures and up? I was so grateful that Kevin was more mature and forthright than the assholes he was forced to work with.

Taking my cues from my well-mannered man, I smiled politely, even though I didn't get the joke. I wasn't really sure I even wanted to "get it," but before I could decide whether to ask what they were talking about, Kevin adjusted his tie, gave them a screw-you-guys look and whisked me away for a slow dance to the so *à propos*, "Hero" by Mariah Cary.

When Kevin did not have his hand on my sashed waist, it was on my bare shoulder. When it was not on my shoulder, it was holding my hand.

"Kevin, stop," I found myself saying constantly, half not meaning it.

"I can't help it. Your neck was screaming, 'Kiss me," he said as he nuzzled.

We had a wonderful evening, perhaps our best, most romantic one ever. He twirled me on the dance floor under the twinkling New York night sky, just as I had envisioned that day on 48th Street during my Saks dress fantasy.

We mingled with other couples. We mingled separately and sneaked peeks at each other from across the crowded room. We stole a moment alone on the bow to kiss in the moonlight.

Then it was time to bid good night to our hosts, "Lovely meeting you; so glad you're feeling better," said the partner, who pulled the short straw and got stuck with farewell duty by the gangplank.

"Er, um, thank you, and thanks for the lovely evening," I said, trying to be gracious and not look as confused as I was. As we reached the dock, I turned to Kevin and wanted to know, "What did he mean 'Feel..."

Kevin grabbed my shoulders squarely, and said, "Did I ever tell you how beautiful you are?"

"Sure, you always say I'm pretty. I'm your Doll Face."

"No, you're beautiful from head to toe."

As we walked toward the cab stand, I acknowledged my new dress that he had paid for.

"So, you get your money's worth?"

"Every cent."

He pulled me close and gave me a long, passionate kiss, like in the movies.

"I'm so proud of you," he whispered. "Not everyone could have done what you did. It took real resolve and commitment. I'm… I...I love you so much."

A major make-out session ensued in the taxi ride home.

"So, what now?" he asked me when we came up for air.

"Now, it's your place to get naked."

"Yeah, right," he laughed, "but no, seriously. I mean do you keep dieting or..."

OK, so much for romancing and seducing me into bed.

"Oh, right. Well, now I'm on maintenance, so I stay within my POINTS allowance, but I only have to weigh in once a month 'cause..."

"What? That's ludicrous. You'll lose your momentum and balloon up again!"

Just then the cab went under the tunnel on the FDR Drive at around 42nd Street, and blackness fell upon my stunned, totally appalled face. He seemed absolutely horrified at the idea that I might gain the weight back.

As we walked through his Upper East Side luxury building's never-ending hallway towards his apartment door, I was preoccupied and therefore silent, as he jabbered away about how work functions can be a chore, but tonight's had been actually worth attending.

When I finally did speak, it was with tears in my heavily shadowed and mascaraed eyes that took me two hours to get right in order to bring out the green from the hazel.

"You told them I was sick," I announced flatly, finally putting together all the comments I had heard that evening.

He got the look that a guilty little boy gets when he swears to his mother that he has not been watching TV. Then she touches the top of the set and it's burning hot.

Busted.

So he did the usual guy thing.

"What? Told who?"

So much for maturity and forthrightness.

"People at your work. You never wanted them to meet the fat chick you were with, no matter how nice or smart or funny she was. So you made excuses. All those 'rubber chicken' dinners? I could have gone. You just didn't invite me. You were ashamed to be seen with me, in front of those officious women and frat boy jackasses no less. Even at my fattest, I still had more poise than they have."

He started doing that Ralph Kramden hum-in-a-hum-in-a-hum-in-a... thing while he concocted an answer. I took the opportunity to add, "And I obviously never made it to Philadelphia because you didn't want your mother to see I couldn't fit into some debutante ball gown."

I punctuated that by turning right back around and walking to the elevator. On my journey, I had time to realize that while I was losing weight, it was so easy for my progress to go undetected by Kevin, not because he was traveling, but because he never really looked at me, never really paid attention.

As the elevator door slid across my now stone face, I could hear Kevin yell, "Doll Face, come back." Then suddenly he was there in front of me, stopping the door from closing completely with his determined, firm hand. As he did, he acknowledged the female resident beside me, whom I had not even noticed, with a just-friendly-enough neighbor nod, "hello."

"Hey," said the sincerely affable neighbor in her teal Juicy track suit on the way to the basement to throw out a mighty packed Hefty drawstring tall kitchen bag.

He ignored her and stared directly at me. "Trish, let's talk about this."

The familiar resident, whom I knew only as 6B, or 6 Bitch, as Kevin used to call her because she played her music too loud, looked at me in disbelief.

"Wow!" She gestured to all of me with her non-garbage-holding hand, "I didn't recognize you. Did you lose weight?"

"Yes," I answered her, looking directly in her face. Then I turned back to Kevin to complete my sentence, "About 175 pounds."

With that, I slapped away Kevin's hand with my gold vintage clutch and the elevator door slid closed, obliterating his "Now that you're hot you're leaving me?" face.

# Chapter 9

## "Trimming the Fat"

The next morning I wasted no time. I rose and shined, then opened my bedroom window and breathed in fresh late spring air, which was warm and revitalizing. I felt light, but now it wasn't from just the weight loss.

I realized that I had held on to Kevin the way I always used to hold on to Kit Kats in a crisis: for dear life. I was a fat chick with a boyfriend, practically unheard of in most social circles. He was young and rich and handsome, and for the love of God, he liked me! He really liked me. I was like the Sally Field of romance.

Even though I believed, and would always believe, that he thought I was a good person who was worth spending time with, at that moment I realized that he probably thought of me more as a friend with benefits than as a girlfriend. But since denial was the name of my game, I had always chosen not to notice that the "benefits" were pretty few and far between and usually initiated by me.

He was so focused on his career and pleasing his family by following the path they had planned for him, there would not have been time to cultivate a real relationship. A real girlfriend whom he intended to get approved by his mother would have put demands on him. He had no time for that. I made no demands. I was too busy being grateful for having a steady guy in my life.

He just never had the heart or the nerve to say that my appearance was not up to snuff with his image or that of his family.

But, he told me in other ways. He never took me to Philadelphia for his monthly, all-day Sunday visits, claiming that he did work on the two-hour limo ride there and back, and he really needed to pay attention to his family when he was there, so he couldn't entertain me. He said I'd be bored, and I went along for that ride, instead of the one to Philly.

Oh, and then there was the small matter of never being invited to the work-related events. I knew people who were always being dragged along to these things and it was like a private joke between them and their boyfriends.

"Remember the time we went to the one at Tavern On The Green and we ended up feeding that tough filet mignon to the stray cats that wandered in from the garden?" was just one of the stories I'd heard couples laughing at. I had always wanted stories like that, even though they were actually silly and quite frankly, not all that funny.

Still…

I had hope that maybe someday I'd have private, albeit silly, shared moments with someone.

I would toss Kevin the fat head as I had tossed my fat clothes. I took last night's green garb which was on his Amex card and turned it into garbage by digging my Rebok-ed heel into one side and pulling up on the other, ripping the dress in two. "Nothing personal, Ms. Rowley." I put both halves in a cardboard Tropicana box I had procured from D'Agostino's and marked "Kevin" on it with a blood red, fat-point Sharpie Marker. I continued to fill it with Kev residue: CDs, books, a New York Knicks T-shirt, a "K" ceramic coffee mug, etc. If it was his, or came from him, it was compost.

My mother called as I cleaned out.

"So how was the party?"

"The party was lovely. I broke up with Kevin."

"Why?" she said in that "oh-no-what-now?" tone that let me know what little peace I brought to her.

"Because it took getting skinny to realize just how thin he really is."

I then explained what had happened, and she said that perhaps I was being too hasty. After all, he had stayed with me while I was fat.

"Oh, I didn't realize that you thought he was doing me a favor for being with me."

"Oh, stop it. You know what I mean. He accepted your imperfections, and now it's your turn to accept his."

Somewhere out there, I knew someone would be nodding a head in agreement with my mother because at first listen, it sounded as though she was making sense.

"This isn't some couple's compromise like, 'You put up with my nail biting and I put up with your leaving the toilet seat up.' "

"Why don't you get on the train, and I'll make you something to eat for lunch and we'll figure out how you two can make up. I feel bad because I've always liked him."

"Well," I said, revolted by the invite to my mother's for her cure-all: food, "you're single and so is he. You can date him." A curt, "I have to go now," ended our conversation.

After hanging up, I headed out onto 10th Street, walked down the block and dumped "Kevin" in the scooper of the garbage truck that was holding up traffic and about to incite a riot of horn-honking impatient New Yorkers.

I decided to "walk that man right out of my hair." I strolled down Bleeker, up Sixth, and over to Greenwich Avenue, where it seemed everyone who was awake was holding someone else's hand. Men and women. Women and women. Men and men. Everyone had someone but me. No wonder I kept a death grip on Kevin. Walking through life solo felt so low.

I called upon my memory banks to cough up what I had read so many times in all the women's magazines about loving yourself and then you wouldn't need anyone else. However, at that moment, in front of Starstruck vintage clothing, I was, as someone from work had pointed out, "half a person" – literally and figuratively.

Not to look so alone, I called Lisa from my cell. She was frying up breakfast for her, Joe and Lil while she listened to my adventure on the low seas.

"Don't worry, they'll be comin' out of the woodwork," I heard her say over the splattering of grease.

"Like termites." I said this as I was being scoped by a bunch of younger guys. Too young. Like high school. I wasn't ready yet for "cougar" status.

"I mean, I think I'll meet somebody," I continued, as I looked in store windows at formfitting clothes usually worn by club kids. One of the storeowners, who was adorned in skulls (jewelry, t-shirt, belt buckle), stopped decorating his display to signal me to come in and try on the slinky outfit with cutouts at the waist. I shook my head and looked as though wearing something that revealing was still unthinkable. Tastewise, it still was, but I walked a little taller across West 4th Street just knowing that I could if I ever wanted to, like on Halloween, maybe.

"How do you meet people?" I was having a dating blackout. Kevin and I had been together for over two years. And our meeting was a fluke.

I had to tell her to hold on a moment, because I would not be able to hear her answer. I had gotten swept into the fray of a street fair on Eighth Avenue.

Rainbow coalition balloons. Much-too-loud garage bands competing for attention, hoping beyond hope that someone from an indy label would stroll by and sign them. Cheap, glittery bangle bracelets to the left of me. Souvlaki and Gyros. Discount "designer" sheets. A booth enticing me to change my long distance carrier, to the right. As I checked out some "genuine" Prada sunglasses, I shouted as I amended my statement.

"Where do you meet people?"

"You're asking me? I'm the married one, remember. I don't know. Wait, join a gym. I heard it on

*Good Day New York*. They said yoga is part of the new singles scene, like aerobics classes were in the '80s."

Just then I passed a Yoga Palace where pedestrians could stand on the street and watch through the window as more meditative souls did downward-facing dog or dog-baying-at-the-moon, or dogs-in-heat, whatever. Nope. Not for me.

"No, but, you know, I've been trying to tone up. My exercise bike though isn't exactly state-of-art. Maybe I'll buy a new one."

"You're not going to meet anyone spinning your wheels in your house," Lisa pointed out.

I passed by a park where a couple was practicing tai chi. I don't think so.

"Buy a real bike or rollerblades or…"

Never. Ever. Ever. Right after my dad had gotten hit by the car, I developed a sort of "street paranoia." I always looked both ways, crossed on the green even if no vehicles were in sight, and didn't like the vulnerability of being atop a few pounds of aluminum with two wheels when others were engulfed by tons of steel on four.

"Nah, I'll end up under a bus. Maybe a gym. I'd never gone before because I never wanted a room full of people to watch my blubber bend and stretch."

"Well that was then and this is now. Did you get the memo on Friday? Image just made a deal with a gym."

Hint, hint employees. All of you now, go Chelsea-fy your bods. Image has an image to maintain.

"Didn't see it. Must be buried under all the other crap on my desk."

"Buff Fitness, I think. Yeah, Buff."

And there it was. Lisa had said the name and conjured it up just as I turned the corner. "We get a discount," she added.

"I'll check it out," I said, right before we ended our call, but not before she let her daughter, Lil, tell her Aunt Trish how she took a ride on her mommy's bike early that morning, and how the afternoon would bring a rousing game of Princess tag.

No wonder Lisa ate pancakes and greasy burgers, but remained steady pound-wise.

She wasn't toned though, as I soon would be.

# Chapter 10

## "Pound for Pound"

They meant business at Buff. *Time Out Magazine* had written them up as the "no bullshit place to work out." The black Lucite reception desk was abuzz. Everyone behind it was toned, fit and standing with shoulders-back perfect posture, or was on the phone or helping an equally toned, fit and standing with shoulders-back perfect posture client with a workout question. I heard the svelte redhead receptionist tell one well-aerobicized woman that she looked "buffalicious."

Since they were three deep at the desk, I decided to wait patiently for my turn and had a look around the shop-'til-you-drop-then-eat-something-healthy waiting area.

Their boutique had every conceivable fitness item of clothing – no cutsie outfits – but "wear this for the ultimate workout" wear. They also sold at-home exercise equipment, so that "no matter where you are, you can be Buff."

Their café was so full of greenery it looked like a rabbit could truly die and go to bunny heaven after feasting on spinach salad with an assortment of vegetables and no-fat dressing. Non-fat fruit smoothies were available to wash it all down. VitaBuff water cost three bucks. I hoped the Image discount extended to all this as well.

Then I saw it and knew I was "home." There was a sign saying that they put together special Weight Watchers salads – only six POINTS.

The hard bods swathed in cotton and spandex and POINTS-conscious menu were tempting, but the tour given by my buff Buff guide was what really sold me.

The equipment looked space age, as though it were designed for the first weightlifter on the moon. The rooms were many, so the classes were small, meaning people were more than an arms length from the person next to them. There were mirrors on every wall and ceiling, so that everywhere you looked there you were in your sweaty, "makin' progress" Buff leotard. And they boasted clean, minimally decorated and soothingly dim massage rooms, as well as private saunas and steam rooms.

These were apparently where you headed to reward yourself after your hard work workout.

I was about to say, "Where do I sign?" when a very young, shapely Asian woman came jogging through the hallway and greeted my tour guide with a high-five, and then sidled up to me.

"Hi, I'm Kim."

"Trish. Hi. Do you work here?"

"No. But I should, heck I should live here, I'm here so much."

My guide smiled and concurred with a nod.

"How are the classes?" I asked, trying to sound like someone who was serious about getting toned, but who had not yet made up her mind if this was the place.

"My advice – personal trainer. I mean then it's all about you. Your body, your workout. It's the best way to get results."

It sounded plausible, and I assumed she'd know; after all, she "lived" there.

My Buff tour guide did not seem at all put out that Kim had taken over her role as seller of all that is Buff. I guess that's because Kim was the best sales tool there is – a satisfied customer.

I signed on the dotted line and said, "Personal trainer it is."

He was tall and handsome and built like, what the boys in my old Bronx neighborhood would have called, a brick shit house. The quintessential Buff man.

Rick, my new personal trainer, reminded me of the lumberjack on the Brawny Paper Towel packages, but instead of a plaid flannel shirt and blue jeans, he wore a tight white tank and spandex shorts both with Buff emblems.

Buffalicious, indeed.

Three days a week for an hour each visit, he worked me.

I whined.

He toned me.

I tantrummed.

He whipped me into shape.

I started seeing results and stopped whimpering.

I began doing my routines without requesting a rest every five seconds and started to fist bump with Rick for my success. I'd also get the thumbs-up from my new gym friend, Kim, when we'd meet up in the locker room.

She had to be the perkiest person I had ever met. Open and friendly. Ingenuous and so pretty. Her long, straight black hair was always in a pony for maximum workout purposes. This showed off her flawless skin, pouty lips and almond-shaped brown eyes.

I kept meaning to ask her what she did for a living, but the people who "lived" and worked out at Buff seemed to never acknowledge their "outside" lives. At Buff, nothing existed but you, your body and becoming buffalicious.

That was OK. I didn't think Kim was at the point in her career where she was actually doing anything worth talking about anyway. I got the impression she was much younger than I had originally thought, and not just because she had baby-soft looking skin. There was something very little girl about her: the squeaky, squeally voice, the "aw shucks" hand gestures. I immediately took a big sister-little sister stance when we spoke.

"How are you tonight Kim?"

"I had a super workout. You?" she would ask, sounding like a teenager.

"I had a good workout as well."

"I just got this leotard," she announced one day very early in our relationship. Then she twirled for me, the way I used to do when I was modeling a frou-frou party dress for my dad. "Do you think it makes me look fat?" she wanted to know.

I gave her my mother's, "Now-don't-be-silly, dear," look, and said, "Oh stop it. You have a very nice body and it looks great on you. Especially the color." The chocolate brown actually went great with her amber coloring. "Now, I don't want to hear you talking like that again."

I was really glad that I had branched out and opened up my world after Kevin and I split. Before that, my life was Image and Kevin. Work and home. Now I had work, home and the gym. Except, work had gotten infinitely more interesting now that Craig let me participate more and interact with the client.

The gym not only was helping my body, but my head too. I felt a lot calmer, less stressed. I was rolling with the punches, going with the flow and handling every little "*Craig wants…*" crisis, that used to have me worshipping at the Milky Way alter, with practically a yawn. Chelsea was good at playing unruffled when something happened, but my in-control reactions were genuine. She couldn't hide how ruffled that made her. Sometimes she looked positively ditsy next to me.

Rick added a different element to the type of people in my life as well.

Down to earth and focused, strong and comfortable, he seemed like his own man. Someone who would never ask, "How high?" when someone like Craig said, "Jump." He would never choose a profession just because it was what his father and grandfather did. Or let the opinions of others sway him. I was developing a crush.

I wanted to live up to his level of dedication to fitness and healthy living, so even when I was home, I'd watched television from my low-tech stationary bike instead of the sofa; chewed gum instead of reaching for a snack; and if I felt stressed from work on a non-Rick night, I'd go into Buff and take a class, use the equipment on my own, or just hang in the health bar and have a salad for dinner.

When I did, Kim always was willing to hang out with me. I'd eat and she'd talk about models and movie stars and whatever or whoever was on the cover of *People*. Half the time, I wasn't even listening. I mean I liked pop culture as much as the next person, but after learning "Who Kate Hudson is dating now!" I was kind of done. No need to dissect the relationship or second-guess whether it would last.

Kim did though. So, I just chewed and nodded my head. Even though she was, I finally found out, twenty-two, she often sounded like a 'tween who was not yet jaded by the reality that celebrities were not as cool, together and glamorous as their publicists make them out to be. She was sweet though, and I really didn't mind the company.

By August, I flitted into Image wearing a floral dress with spaghetti straps, which gave all a bird's eye view of my flab-free arms. This was not the customary uniform of the agency account executive, but my new self-possession cheered me on so, that I began to believe I was no longer the run-of-the-mill AE. There was no longer a need for me to act or dress as though I were.

The confidence I had gained, as well as the poise I'd garnered, from adding muscle to my slender frame had gotten kicked up a notch. Make that two notches.

Lisa and I bumped into each other in the coffee room.

I grabbed for a bottled water, standing a little farther away from the fridge than normally someone would. This made it necessary for me to stretch my arm out, making it easy to see how toned I had become.

"Hey, babe," said my pal. "Look at that definition in those arms. And your legs look amazing too. I'm impressed."

"Thank you."

"Great dress. Goin' out after work or something?" she asked as she leaned against the counter.

"Nope, just thought I'd dress the way I feel – like a blossoming flower," I responded, thinking that I sounded lighthearted and poetic.

Lisa looked at me like, "Yeah, right, nobody really talks like that," as she nabbed one of the last Dunkin' Donuts powdered thing from a box that had been sitting on the counter for the better part of the morning.

"Did you hear, Chelsea is sick. Like pneumonia or something," conspired my friend in a you-didn't-hear-it-from-me whisper.

"I know," I said, trying not to sound like I just got an early Christmas present. "I have to help Byron run the account." Since we were in a public area, I called upon all my resolve in order to contain myself. I was so happy Chelsea was infirmed. I didn't want her to die or anything, well...OK, no-no, not die, just perhaps get a relapse so she would be out of the way until, I don't know, retirement age, maybe?

"You go, girl," said Lisa, as she swept some powered sugar from the lapel of her funeral-colored suit jacket. I had never really noticed what a conservative, boring dresser she was.

Right before we went our separate ways, I felt compelled as someone who had changed the error of her dietary ways, to gesture disapprovingly towards Lisa's glazed, custard-filled eyesore that at one point in my life I would have seen as a luscious treat. The sight of it was now sickening.

"Do you know how many POINTS that is?" I inquired.

Lisa looked me right in eyes, took a guiltless, long, luxurious bite and smiled with her sugarcoated lips together as she chewed.

I just smiled at how silly she looked, and shook my head at how stupid she was to put that poison in her body.

That evening Rick put me through my body-transforming paces.

"So, how'd you get into this? GRUNT. You just like torturing people? MOAN." I semi-flirted as I huffed and puffed. I wanted to get inside his head. Actually, I wanted to get inside his pants, but not in a superficial, one-night-stand way. He seemed like a "real relationship" kind of guy.

Serious and professional, friendly, without a trace of a "player" vibe, Rick was who I used to stare at when he'd tell me to "find a spot to focus on," as I was doing my routines. His features were chiseled, yet welcoming. His black mass of hair was short on the sides with a dollop of curls on top. He looked like my mother's favorite old time actor, Victor Mature.

And I liked that everyone liked Rick. He was genuinely helpful and just plain nice. When I found out that he hailed from Wisconsin, well, he had me. Being a born and bred city girl, I always bought into the John Cougar Mellencamp portrayal of Midwesterners, with their cows and cornstalks and in this case, cheese, being just really good people. I deserved a really good person. Good guy, as it were. I wondered if it was OK to date your trainer or was it a taboo like a coed sleeping with a professor?

"Cut it out," he barked when Rick thought I wasn't giving my leg presses my all. "Gimme three more."

As I said, he was serious.

"I bet you were one of those kids who put the gerbil in the microwave to watch it explode," I offered as I moved on to the next station in my program.

"Too much talk; not enough squat."

Later on, when I was released from workout prison, I went for nourishment at the Buff health bar. As I washed down my specially concocted Weight Watchers VeggieBuff salad with an 8oz. VitaBuff, I noticed a visibly thinner Kim was wandering about drinking a Diet Coke with lemon, and as always flipping through *People*. I signaled for her to join me.

When we first met, she had a full face. About my height, her body was slender yet curvy. Kim made a great advertisement for the gym: "Real bodies. Real firm," I could hear one of my copywriters reciting.

Now the curves had seemed to diminish and she was bordering on flat chested.

"I don't care what anybody says. Lara Flynn Boyle is not too thin."

OK, if you say so.

I just chuckled. It was as though we were picking up a conversation where we had left it off two weeks ago. Ours had become a very easy friendship. We never made plans; we just sort of met up. "See ya when I see ya," I used to say when it was time to say good-bye. I realized that she was the only person I knew whom I didn't feel pressured around. There was no talk of jobs, schedules, or appointments. Always some superficial, light and breezy conversation about what some actress wore on the red carpet or a new lipstick that puffed out your lips so you wouldn't need Botox. It was a very non-taxing relationship, and that suited me just fine. There was also no pressure for party manners or getting-to-know-you small talk. Kim had a way of treating people like they were close friends. So, I jumped right on the familiarity bandwagon.

"Aren't you going to eat anything?" I asked her, sounding, as usual when I was around her, like my mother.

"Sure, I'm gonna eat the lemon," she shrugged like a smart aleck teen, and with that, she fished it out of her soda with her boney fingers. "Kim wants to stay slim. I'm a zero you know."

"What?" I wasn't sure what question I wanted answered first. Why she thought a lemon was eating. Why she referred to herself in the third person? Or what a zero was? She chose the third one first.

"Size zero. What size are you?"

"Well, I was a four, but my clothes are feeling a little roomy, so I guess maybe now I'm a two.

Kim just shrugged again and added a smirk as she sucked on her lemon, admiring all the *People* people. "Well, I'm a zero."

Well, OK, whatever makes you feel like a "ten."

"Yeah, I noticed you look skinnier than when we first met."

"I love you for noticing," she oozed as she blew me a kiss across the table.

"I actually didn't realize you were trying to lose weight. I thought you were just here to get toned, like I am. I mean you've lost your curves."

"By curves, you mean fat."

"No. I meant what I said. 'Curves'."

"Hey, you say 'potato' and I say... 'Get those carbs away from me.' Ha, ha, ha." While she sat and laughed at her own bad joke, I smirked and said a prayer thanking God that I am an only child. I could not have grown up listening to this kind of silly crap from a younger sibling at the dinner table every night.

"So, aside from your exercise routine here, what kind of diet are you on?"

"Oh, it's my own. I made it up. I don't eat breakfast. I have a light lunch. And, you know, a little something for dinner."

"Like a lemon?" I condescended.

Kim slurped the remnants of her melted crushed ice through her straw, went back to her magazine article about a town that collectively lost three thousand pounds, and shrugged me off – again – the way I used to do to my mother when I was a petulant fifteen-year-old.

"Don't try to make me fat," she singsonged, not looking up from her weight-related reading.

I laughed and rolled my eyes. Isn't that how people deal with little sisters?

# Chapter 11

## "Love Handles"

I wandered through Barney's that Saturday afternoon. I browsed alongside the rich and the beautiful. I finally felt comfortable in my own skin. Relaxed because I actually had a choice of the clothes I could wear. The decision wasn't made for me by how generous someone had elected to cut their pattern, but by how generous I could afford to be to myself.

I caught my reflection in the long, tall mirror (my God, even the décor in this place was statuesque) and stopped to admire and be amazed by my now flat belly.

The sales assistant I had enlisted had gone in search of a pair of Theory tapestry pants, displayed on a mannequin. They looked more like a work of art than an article of clothing.

"Here's that size two, but I'm afraid there's no fitting room available at the moment."

I looked at her and announced smugly, "I don't need to try them on. They'll fit." And they did. Later that day, when I got home and tried them on in my bedroom, I couldn't believe how perfectly they swaddled my body. It was as though they had been custom made.

I transformed, if only in my imagination, the strip of oak parqué floor that ran from the door to the window of my bedroom into a fashion show runway. To complement my new size two's, I put on Jimmy Choo black peep-toe slingbacks with a four-inch heel. I had treated myself a couple of months ago, as per Weight Watchers' advice, to reward myself for my accomplishments. My JCs were for all the diligence it took to stay the course at Buff.

I threw all what was left of my weight back, flung my legs out and strutted my boudoir's imaginary stage like a model. No, make that a supermodel. No, a superdupermodel. Like Janice Dickenson, I'd coined a new model moniker.

I considered wearing this outfit to our next *TREND* meeting so they could see how stylish and well, *TREND*-worthy I was. I was becoming high profile on the account, since poor Chelsea had had a relapse (prayers do get answered) and her ETA back to Image was uncertain.

Life had certainly changed for me. While I did the *New York Sunday Times* crossword and sipped on an unsweetened ice tea at an outdoor café on Bleeker Street the next afternoon, I went to take a pen from my purse when my pencil point broke. Sitting next to me were two European looking men, who resembled the proverbial French lovers in every foreign film I had ever seen. They must have thought that I was hunting around for a cigarette and instantly flicked their lighters at me when I surfaced with my find.

I had grown accustomed to being greeted at the gym with a rousing, "You look buffalicious today." I guess Rick started liking the results of his handiwork, and me as well. He began inviting me to celebrate my stamina and determination with a PowerBuff Shake at the health bar *après*-workout.

Kim never came over to interfere; instead, she'd walk by a million times and give me the thumbs-up when she thought Rick wasn't looking. I got a kick out of her. She was such a little goofball, she made me feel more like a grownup.

"You were heavy?" I repeated his adjective to make sure I had heard him correctly.

"I wasn't heavy. I was the fat kid," emphasized Rick.

"Get. Outta. Here."

"You're right, I'm lying. I wasn't the fat kid. I was the big, fat kid."

"I bet you were cute," I teased.

Just then Rick took a photo from his yellow, nylon sports wallet.

I stared at the clearly ancient Polaroid of him in a blue and white striped t-shirt, ill-fitting and snug blue-jean shorts; a triple scoop chocolate, vanilla and strawberry ice cream cone in one hand and a bag of popcorn in the other. He was standing in front of a huge sign that read: State Fair. The closest I ever came to one of those is when I saw an Elvis movie by the same name. As I stared at the photo of this young, portly stranger in a strange land, I believe I could make out a cow and a few pigs in the background. He looked almost identical to the character a pre-teen Jerry O'Connell played in the movie, *Stand By Me*.

When I realized that I had been transfixed with my mouth wide open, I became self-conscious and decided I should say something. "This is you? Sweet Jesus, I can't believe you were so enormous." Yes, my body may have slimmed down, but my mouth was still big and fat.

The only thing that saved me was the fact that my reaction was so unoriginal. "Yeah, that's what everybody says, more or less. I carry this shot around so I remember what I could become again if I don't take care of myself. By the time I got to senior year in high school, my nickname was "Thick Rick." Needless to say, I didn't go to the prom."

"I went to mine. Senior year was a thin year for me. Trust me when I say, you didn't miss anything."

"Just as well, I don't think there would have been enough material in the western world to have created the tux. In fact, Omar the Tent Maker would not have had in his possession enough fabric to cover my rear, thighs, paunch and the always-attractive man breasts." He saw he was amusing me, so kept up his riff. "And if by some act of God, Omar could oblige, I would have walked into the school gym looking like the lead in *The Attack of the Giant Penguin*.

My boisterous laugh made me push away from the table and cover my face. I looked away for a moment to check myself in one of the club's many mirrors just to make sure none of my strawberry PowerBuff shake was shooting out my nose.

The last thing I needed was to look back at Rick and see that two women, known around the club as "The

Bombshells," were about to explode on the scene. Like Kim, they too "lived" at Buff. Unlike her, I think they spent more time strutting around in their shimmery and one-size-too-small workout wear than actually ever doing their workouts.

"Hi, Rick," baby talked B1 with a bleached blonde Farrah Fawcett circa Charlie's Angels hair toss.

"Hey there, Ricky," singsonged B2 as she pressed her upper arms against her upper body to make her *faux* breasts pop out even more than they did naturally.

Don't mind me, I'm just sitting here right next to him.

He barely looked at them.

"Hi," he said as he took a swig of his vanilla PowerBuff.

I'm sure they would never accept that a member of the male species would have the restraint to resist them, so they acted as though they were playing hard to get by wiggling away with a bye-bye wave made famous by two-year olds like Lisa's daughter, Lil.

Even though he was shaking his head in a disgusted kind of way, he was still watching them walk off.

"Other clients?" I said to bring his attention back to my side of the table.

"Nah, they just hang out here. I don't even know if they'd know how to work up a sweat."

I couldn't help but notice the two bombshells watching Rick from afar.

"Well, they probably would if they could workout with you. Do you give a *ménage-à-trois* discount?"

I thought that was good enough for a chuckle. He just stared pensively out the window past the mob scene that is 7th Avenue South, and into the distance.

"They're the girls I thought I could never get back in the day, and now I don't want."

I just stared admiringly at him. I thought, "I've finally found a true 'good guy' who appreciates when people take care of the outside, but who's only really interested in seeing what's inside.

## Chapter 12

### "If She Turns Sideways, You Can't See Her"

The next day, I fantasized about Rick the whole train ride to Westchester.

Mother's birthday party was in full swing when I arrived. Aunts, uncles and cousins from the tri-state area showed up. Neighbors she had gotten friendly with since she'd moved there going on sixteen years ago. And friends who were so well loved and had been around so long, they were more like family. Everyone showed up to honor Mom.

I loved my mother's yearly *soirée*. Because it was autumn, the weather was too crisp to have it outside, but it was nice enough that we could leave both the front and side doors open to keep the fresh clear air circulating.

I walked into the kitchen without being noticed.

"Where's Trish?" I overheard my aunt say.

"She's on her way," my mother answered.

"How is she doing with her weight?"

"Great."

My mother's support and acknowledgment overwhelmed me. So much so, that I snuck up behind both Mother and Aunt Emma and gave them the thin girl's version of a bear hug.

"Well, I'm here and... here," I smiled as I handed my mother three tickets to the Broadway show, *Chicago*. Obviously, one was for her, one for me and the third for my aunt. "To get such good seats I had to buy them for months from now. Mark your calendars. I'll take us to dinner first."

They both accepted my kisses and gift, then my mother started in with me.

"Did you say hello to everybody?"

"I said hello to everyone, and now I'm here to say hello to you." I gave my mother another little squeeze.

"Can you eat anything? I don't want you to ruin your diet," Mom worried.

So much for support and acknowledgment. Her new obsession with my new appearance was offending me on more levels than I could have ever imagined. I felt like a recovering drunk who she feared would fall off the wagon at the slightest provocation. *Quick hide the rubbing alcohol!*

Did she really believe I was that weak? My twenty-ninth birthday was right around the corner – four months away in January – yet she made me feel like a child who still could not take care of herself. I had been doing this weight loss program for over a year. I had made incredible progress. I had committed to an exercise regimen that would have sent lesser mortals into the emergency ward with chest pains; yet she didn't think I would come to a party prepared to accommodate my changed eating habits?

To top it off, I had explained the Weight Watchers plan a million…no exaggeration, a million times. I could eat anything. Anything, as long as I stayed within my range of eighteen to twenty-five POINTS per day.

Technically, even though it would be a true, artery-hardening, nutritional nightmare, I could have one egg, two slices of bacon and two slices of Wonder bread toast (six POINTS) for breakfast, a slice of pizza (nine POINTS) for lunch and a Whopper Jr. (ten POINTS) for dinner, yet remain true to the diet. When was she going to "get with the program" and understand so she would stop asking me?

"So, can you?" she reiterated.

I took a deep breath so that she would know how exasperating she was being. "I told you. I. Can. Eat. Anything. As. Long. As. I. Stay. Within. My. POINTS." I felt like Mr. Kotter trying to teach the ever-remedial Sweathogs.

Since it was her birthday and she did not want to get into an argument with me, she waved me off with, "OK, Patricia. You're a grown woman. You can feed yourself." And left the kitchen with a tray of two-POINTS-apiece *hors d'oeuvres* to pass among her guests.

I must say, this woman must have been a caterer in another life. She had opened the dining room table to accommodate both leaves. Every inch of it was covered with a plate chockfull of you-name-it. There were snack tables opened and scattered about the room, which also offered her company something to nosh on. The cold cuts notwithstanding, she made it all herself -- each deviled egg, stuffed mushroom and clam oreganata. There was a giant pan of lasagna, as well as a pork roast and roast beef. Enough mixed green salad with black olives, pimento olives, cherry tomatoes and artichoke hearts tossed in that one would think my mother was feeding a small village of vegetarians. And what party would be complete without the standard assortment of junk: chips, pretzels, peanuts and Chex mix. She still journeyed back to our old 'hood near Little Italy's Arthur Avenue for Italian pasties.

No wonder I had grown up with eating issues.

My aunt, God knows why, took the liberty of making a dish for me. She handed me the Chinette plate with a small sampling of each food.

I wanted to scream. What was I, twelve? How was this helping? She didn't know how to measure? I don't even like clams. Jesus Christ.

"Oh, no. Not like that," I rebuffed as I snatched the plate from her and stopped short of dumping the whole thing in the white Hefty tall kitchen bag that lined the trash can.

I then went into my oversized Kate Spade black nylon tote and took out a small Weight Watchers issue food scale. I went into the dining area and placed it on the side, serving table my mother had reserved for beverages. Oblivious to all around me, I proceeded to measure small portions of different, select dishes being offered.

My mother came up behind me and said in her low, embarrassed voice, the one she used to use when, in high school, I'd insist upon wearing ripped jeans and a jean jacket and embroidered peasant blouse to a family Christmas party or Baptism. "Are you nuts? It's a party."

"And? That means I shouldn't be careful? Five minutes ago, you were asking whether I could eat anything. Well, here's your answer. I can, in measured amounts." With that I gestured like a *Price Is Right* prize model to the scale.

Because she had distracted me from what could have almost looked like the performance of a science experiment, some tomato sauce got on the cuff of my black tweed Donna Karan peplum jacket, that I practically stole at a sample sale it was so cheap. It went with anything and everything. Every time I had it on and got in a yellow cab, I actually imagined myself in one of Donna's ads.

In its very short life with me, the jacket had become a well-loved item. I knew I could never replace it, except maybe if I got lucky on eBay, so I went out of my way to preserve it. At work I never left it draped over the back of my chair and always took it off to eat my lunch. I checked it at restaurants.

"Oh, look what you made me do."

So offended by my disdain, Aunt Emma, who had been watching the exchange with my mother, just tsked and walk away from me in disgust.

I took off my jacket to reveal a sleeveless T-shirt. I went to the kitchen sink to wash off the sauce, and I sensed someone behind me.

"Dear God, you're so skinny." Mother's timbre was shock and awe.

"I'm not skinny. Olive Oyl is skinny. I'm trim and toned. I work out with a trainer. Remember, I told you?"

"Don't get too thin. I don't want you to get sick."

I was so beside myself, I took my prize possession jacket and threw in on the yellow and white tile linoleum.

"You make me crazy, you know that," I shouted with tears in my eyes. I could hear the chatter from the living and dining rooms lull. "First I'm too fat. Now I'm too skinny. You find fault no matter what."

"I'm just saying..."

To show her just how uninterested I was in what she was "just saying," I threw out the plate of food I'd just measured and punctuated it with, "I've lost my appetite."

I picked up my jacket, and smoothed it out after I had it back on. I rejoined the party and tried to overcompensate for the disruption by being solicitous, offering to refill drinks and picking up the dish of salty, fatty, POINTS-filled peanuts and offering them to those of our friends and relatives who still ate every meal as though it were their last.

I gladly took compliments about how great I looked and fielded questions about how I did it, hoping some of these people would get inspired to jump on the weight loss bandwagon. When someone would tell me how nice I looked and I knew my mother was in earshot, I'd turn, look her in the face and give her a withering, "told-you-so look." *Happy Birthday to you.*

# Chapter 13

## "Chewing the Fat"

The next evening, in our first out-of-gym hang, Kim and I mingled with the after-work executive crowd mixed with model-types at Bette, the cool, downtown eatery that always gets much buzz on *Page Six*. Now that I had adopted her as my little sister, I wanted to show her the New York City scene that most young people can't afford to see because they are still on the diet known as entry-level salary.

I felt bad having blown off Lisa. "Hey, my husband's taking Lil to his mother's. I'm solo tonight. Want to grab a bite like old times?" But this place was fun and hot and through a contact at *TREND* I was able to wrangle a reservation. Honestly, I just didn't want to waste it on someone as suburban and plain as Lisa. Don't get me started on her boring business suits from Bolton's.

I found it laughable when I heard her say that she worked on a fashion account. I mean I know underwear can be fashionable, but Hanes? It's not like she worked on Victoria's Secret or anything.

There was also another issue for me. It was getting hard for me to watch Lisa eat. Her dietary behavior reminded me of what I used to be. Grabbing for donuts or whatever, even fruit, on platters in meetings, when I wasn't even hungry; paying no mind to portion sizes; running to the snack cart like one of

Pavlov's dogs when the vendor announced his 3 p.m. arrival with the ring of a bell.

I guessed that, because she already had a husband, she didn't care if she let herself go or not. No, I could not extend an invitation to Lisa to dine at Bette. I hate to say this about my dear friend, but she'd have embarrassed the sensible eating and chic me. I knew, however, that Kim would really enjoy and appreciate being with the beauteous and voguish.

Kim and I both ordered the roasted chicken (lemon/butter sauce on the side) with a green vegetable. However, Kim seemed to be doing more people watching than eating.

"So it worked to your benefit. You ended up not eating all that fatty "mom" party food. Is that Naomi Campbell? Over there, by the bar? I think I'm thinner than she is."

I turned to scope out the supermodel. "I can't see, Tom Ford's in the way. So, anyway, you're saying I should thank my mother for aggravating me?"

"She saved you calories."

Some see the world as black and white. Others see shades of gray. Kim only sees it in calories. I probably was not one to talk, since I had learned to see the world in POINTS.

"I guess," I answered, still trying to figure out if saving calories had been worth losing my temper at my mother's house.

"So how's work?" I said as I sighed to shake off birthday party residue. I also changed the subject to try and lift our conversation out of the usual diet/who's thin/what size she wears doldrums as well as take our friendship to the next level; to start sharing interests and events in our lives that were not specific to Buff, or who was on the cover of this week's *People*.

"Um...fine, whatever," said Kim, who was still distracted with model fever.

"What do you do, by the way?" I stammered, realizing that she had never said, and that I had never bothered to ask. In fact, she had never inquired as to my profession either.

"That is Naomi Campbell. What size do you think she is?" asked Kim. Dear God, I realized that Lisa was not the only one who had the potential to embarrass me at Bette.

"I...um...don't know what size Naomi Campbell could be. So, did I ever tell you I work in advertising as the Account Executive on the *TREND* Magazine account?" I said this knowing that would get my dinner "date" to actually make dinner conversation with me, as well as eye contact.

"No, really?"

Got her. "Yes. It's actually very exciting. We're ptiching them a new campaign and because the Account Supervisor – this brainless, Victoria's Secret type – is sick, I've taken over as Acting Supervisor. We're hoping to sell them this campaign where..."

"Are there parties? Like fashion parties? Can you bring me? Are the models there? Have you ever met any? Are they nice? Do they ever say what they eat? Do they ever share what tricks they use to stay thin? Do they leave the party and throw up in the bathroom? Do they ever bring rock stars as their dates?"

*Dear God. "Can I go to the prom with you and your boyfriend in the limo? Can I? Can I? Can I? Can I get a prom dress too, even though I'm nine?"*

"Well, so far there haven't been any parties, just lots of work, so..."

"But if there are parties with models, will you bring me? Will you? Will you?" She was a sweet girl, but seriously, all I could think was, "Grow up."

I mean everyone likes to hear about models and movie stars; look at what they're wearing to the Oscars; get a glimpse of how they live and where they hang out or shop; but then you close the magazine or turn off *Access Hollywood* and get on with your life. I was beginning to get the impression, though, that Kim might not have had much of one.

"Sure." I said this to save myself the trouble, the way my mother used to placate my incessant badgering with, "Sure, sure. You can write the Easter Bunny a letter inviting him to Sunday dinner. I'll make sure to set another place."

I also chose to mollify her because I believed it was the only answer she would accept. When she responded to my admission that I did business among the fashionistas with such scary intensity, it made me feel threatened. Who would say no to someone who had a look in her eyes that screamed, *If you say you won't take me, I'll have to stalk you, then kill you and assume your identity so I can use your ticket to get into the party. Sorry.*

That night, I found out that outside of the controlled gym environment, not only did I have little in common with Kim, but little patience for her as well. I was a tad bit uncomfortable around my little sister/ friend.

Well, our evening wasn't going to last forever, so I figured I'd just try to be gracious and get through it, as one does when entertaining an "outta towna" or an important client.

I settled into the comfort of the mundane and safe. "So the food is good, isn't it? This chicken is really amazing."

Kim, who had not touched her meal and was craning her neck to see over the crowd, responded, "Yeah, it's good."

"How would you know?" My mother's voice came out of my mouth.

"I had some."

"No you didn't." Why am I doing this? I thought.

"Yes. I. Did," she insisted. "Not 'cleaning my plate' is how Kim stays slim."

Again with the third person reference. "No seriously."

Kim looking practically wild-eyed burst out with, "What do you care? You're not trying to make me fat are you?"

I looked around and saw people looking. This is the kind of chic New York restaurant where no one will tolerate anyone who doesn't belong. Acting out in a hot eatery where everyone is trying to prove how cool they are will get you thrown out.

"OK. Please lower your voice. Now think about it. Why would I want to make you fat?" Check please.

"A little 'size' envy, Miss Two-Not-A-Zero like me?"

More patrons were starting to look. "Keep. Your. Voice. Down. Now, you're kidding right?"

The waitress came over and asked if everything was all right, which is a polite way of saying, perhaps you should think of leaving soon. After I assured her that there was no problem, she offered reticently to recite the dessert menu.

"No just the check, thanks."

Kim noticed that "supermodels" along with those diners who were just "super-looking" might be watching her outbursts, so she gained – albeit insincerely – her composure. "Of course, I am," she said as she smiled sweetly. "I'm kidding and um, just not as hungry as I thought."

"You can ask them to wrap it for later," I suggested, like my raised-during-the-depression grandmother.

"Oh, right. I will."

I finished my meal and insisted upon taking care of the entire bill. I was not being generous; just paying for my mistake.

When we finally departed, we said our "good nights," and when I turned to cross the street, I happened to look back, and saw Kim slam-dunk her doggie bag in the nearest garbage can.

# Chapter 14

## "Big Chance"

With Rick's voice always in my head, I made it through the holiday season as well as New Year's without gorging, pigging out, and gaining from party food.

He taught me to eat sensibly before each *fête*, when I was there to allow myself two *hors d'oeuvres* and one wine; then switch to sparkling water. If there was a fruit platter, I could have as much as I wanted. I actually think that for the first time in my life I didn't just maintain, but lost weight over Christmas.

Shortly after life got back to normal, it was my birthday. As Tuesdays go, it was pretty eventful on the work front with getting ready to get our big *TREND* campaign presentation underway.

After the ruckus I had caused at my mother's celebration, combined with the fact that we got into another little can-you-eat-that-on-your-diet-don't-get-too-skinny discussion on Christmas, I was surprised she even called to wish me many happy returns.

Lisa and Byron wanted to throw me the usual conference room party, but I asked them not to. Honestly, I didn't want to waste POINTS on a piece of Carvel cake. Carvel was one of our clients, so Craig made it the agency's mandatory party dessert. And I didn't want to share it with forty-nine people who were fine to work with, but with whom I really didn't want to commemorate the day I entered the world.

I worked out with Rick at my usual time. I told him it was my birthday. He congratulated me with one of his big, pearly smiles, but turned back immediately into my taskmaster and told me there'd be no special treatment. He put me through my usual paces, then let me go five minutes early, "As my gift to you." He then made sure to let me know, he'd get the five back by adding them on to next time.

As I left, I nodded "Hi," to Kim on the treadmill. I would not mention that it was my special day. One of my New Year's Resolutions was to never again share another bit of personal information with her, so she didn't know there was anything to celebrate. We would remain gym pals. I would give her someone to talk to about whether Paris Hilton looks good in pink, but that's it. I would have cut her loose, period, but there was just something about her that worried me. I felt a need to stay close, at least physically.

And so, twenty-nine came and went very subdued. And that was OK. I went home and watched television. I was a year away from thirty, yet looked and felt better than I had when I was twenty-five, a fat year. I could have actually worn – no, modeled – the styles they were describing on *E! Fashion File*.

*Happy Birthday to me.*

The following Saturday after my afternoon workout, I stood under the black and red striped awning outside of Buff waiting for the bleak winter rain to let up.

The drops were coming down like bullets targeting the pavement. Not wanting to become a victim of a stray, I resigned myself to just standing there for however long it took for things to let up.

Then appeared my knight in shining spandex. Rick exited the gym waving his black saber, which doubled as a giant umbrella. It was the kind the guys on the street sell for twenty big ones, because when you flick it open, you and a family of five could fit comfortably – and dryly – underneath.

"Hey," said Rick. I loved when a man spoke to me first.

"Have a good night."

"No umbrella?

"Forgot it."

"No cabs?"

"Oh c'mon. Cabs? In New York? When it's raining? I didn't realize you were religious and believed in miracles." With that, the wind sent a giant raindrop whipping into my left eye. As I rubbed and then blinked to focus, just to make sure I had not been blinded, I finished in all seriousness with, "I'm not too far, anyway, I'll just wait 'til it lets up, then walk."

"Here, let me walk you home," he said, while positioning his umbrella so only half covered him and the empty half welcomed me.

It was he, not the umbrella that I wanted to be under. I accepted the offer, not having felt this protected since my father was alive.

We hurried down the splashy getting-dark streets, making conversation that was easy to make since Rick was so unpretentious and agreeable. I was in mid-grin at some story he was telling about a client who dubbed him "The Ayatollah Bodybuilder," when we passed a West Village neighborhood dive with Kevin sitting by the window accompanied by Modelizer Bob. *What no human mannequins to drink with? Bob must be slipping.* I had seen Bessie on the *Style Network* a few months ago being interviewed about her new line of plus-size lingerie called "Romance Plus..." When the commentator asked who she would be wearing it for, Bessie mugged and winked, then confided that she was still waiting for the right one to remove it for. I wondered if she had told Bob to beat it in French.

The "ex" and I made uh-oh-oh-no eye contact.

Kevin, still preppy and open-faced friendly, as always, played to his rep of "good guy." He gave a wave.

I, still stinging from feeling like the charity case he had dated yet would not introduce to people until I was no longer unpleasingly plump, turned my head and slipped my hand through Rick's massive, Rock of Gibraltar upper arm as to give the impression that we were "together." He didn't seem to mind.

When we were out of Kevin's sight, I unslipped my hand and grabbed Rick's boulder of a forearm, tugging slightly as a signal for him to run.

"Oh, Christ hurry."

"Are you cold or..."

"I just saw someone I was hoping never to see again."

We finally reached the entrance of my pre-war apartment building and gave the umbrella a well-deserved rest by huddling under the sprawling hunter green awning.

"Was it a hit man?" Rick joked. "You don't owe the mob do you?"

I wanted to laugh and show him that I appreciated his humor, and that he had been a good sport, but instead I began to tear up.

"Trish? Oh, no. What?"

"An old boyfriend. Actually the newest old boyfriend. We were together when I was fat...and he did care for me, but only behind closed doors. Then when I lost weight, he couldn't wait to parade me around like his prized pig."

My new good guy swept me in his sculpted guns and rocked me gently as he whispered, "I'm sorry. I'm so sorry." Then he took out his wallet and once again showed me his State Fair photo. "I'm the same person. But people treat me differently now that I don't look like I could eat ice cream, popcorn and them all in one bite."

As he replaced the picture in its yellow compartment, he continued, "I told you, I don't want the people who would not have given me the time of day 'before,'" making air quotations with his fingers. "You're better to be away from him." With that, Rick took my single chin, looked into my eyes and kissed me.

We kissed until we realized we were drawing a crowd from others who had sought refuge under the awning; so we decided to move our romantic epiphany upstairs.

As soon as the key unlatched the lock, Rick scooped me up and carried me over the threshold like a bride. I pointed to the bedroom. There was no reason to pretend that was not the reason he was there. Offering a beverage would have seemed clumsy rather than gracious.

"My God, you are so beautiful," he said after he undressed me.

I was speechless, so I let my body do the talking. I maneuvered on top so I could show off my lean physique courtesy of the man himself.

"You are the sexiest woman I have ever been with."

To show my appreciation for his admiration, we did it every which way to Sunday.

As we lay cuddling well into the wee hours, I savored every memory of our lovemaking, and dwelled in particular on our oral pleasures. As always, I wondered how many POINTS that cost me.

# Chapter 15

## "Living Off the Fat of the Land"

For the first time in my life everything had gelled. I had pride in my appearance, I had a guy I really connected with, and my job was going great. Chelsea had not returned to the office. *Wow, making a novena really works.* I was so busy living my life that I didn't have time to talk about it *ad nauseum*.

"Hey, stranger. How's it going?" Lisa asked, as she sauntered into my office. We had not had lunch, kibitzed on the phone or schmoozed over an afternoon cup o' Joe in what seemed like forever. This day was not the day though for a reconciliation. I was too absorbed in looking at .jpegs of models we were considering for our campaign presentation to even properly acknowledge her.

"Christ, I've never been so busy. Look at this shot of Elle McPherson. They need a two-page spread for her legs alone."

Lisa chuckled and wanted for me to join her, but c'mon, who had time? But, of course, I did have time to think of myself.

"I like how her legs go in like that at the thigh. I think I'll tell Rick to work on that with me. You know, maybe there's a special squat I can do or something."

"Right," Lisa said, not quite sure if I was serious or joking. "So um, any word on Chelsea?"

As I clicked to enlarge one slide and discarded another, I noted, "Gone."

"What hap… ?"

"I just found out this morning. While she was sick, I kind of took over her job and the client likes me better. So when she was ready to return, the only job at her level to come back to was on the Toilette Fresh account. She said, "'No,' and quit."

"Can't blame her I guess," Lisa shrugged.

Lisa indicated a young woman chatting with others in the hall. "Did you meet the new Assistant Account Executive, Sarah?"

I gave a quick peek. She was about twenty-two, with a white Peter Pan collar blouse and straight shapeless navy skirt, 'do-free hair and no make-up. And I don't mean the "no makeup" makeup look. I mean absolutely no cosmetics whatsoever. This was not the image of Image. What was Craig thinking? She could also have shed a few pounds; after age nine, baby fat is embarrassing. I gave a dismissive, "Please." I was finally in my element with models and other hip, stylish and toned people; like I had any interest in the Bo Peeps of the world?

"What? She seems sweet," Lisa defended. "Craig wants her to work on each account for a while, to see where she fits."

"Well, she doesn't fit with me," I said as I rolled my eyes. "I mean look at her. I can't bring *that* to *TREND*."

I printed out one of the shots of the model that I liked best and held it up to the natural light coming in from my window. It would probably be the last time I ever saw that view of Manhattan, since I was moving later that afternoon into Chelsea's supervisor three-window pad that faced uptown.

While I ignored her and admired the shot of supermodel Carolyn Murphy, Lisa let loose, "You snotty bitch...listen to yourself."

I put down the photo and addressed her accusation. "I'm not being snotty or a bitch. I'm being honest. Even if she doesn't look like she should be in the damn magazine, the least she could do is look like she reads it."

"You know, I was going to ask you if you were free for lunch, but..."

"Can't. I'm meeting Rick."

"You work out at lunch now, too?"

I pushed my work aside, took out my new Prada bag bestowed upon me by my new pal at *TREND* who oversaw the accessories closet, and began to apply lipstick. "No, we're having lunch. We're seeing each other."

"You're dating your trainer?"

"Don't say it like, 'You're dating your boss?' He's a guy. We met at the gym. And he's great."

"Hope so. You never said...You didn't even tell me. So, are we friends anymore or what?"

"Of course, but your friend happens to be really busy."

I walked out of the office in the midst of our conversation and she shadowed me, partly because there was no point in staying in my office if I wasn't there, but mostly because she couldn't believe I was that rude. I guess she thought that if she kept the conversation going, I'd have a chance to redeem myself.

"So is he…"

"He's amazing and we have lots in common and he appreciates me the way I am and compliments me and…"

With that, we reached the elevator where Lisa interrupted with a clenched jaw, "Can't wait to meet your new guy."

"Maybe I can get him to give you a free session," I replied as I gave my friend's upper arm a pinch. "You could use it."

Lisa looked at me in disbelief and was about to utter a choice word, but the elevator door closed across her pretty face.

# Chapter 16

## "Big Shot"

"So this weekend is the play you got us tickets for at my birthday. Where are we going to eat?" requested my mother.

"Sorry I can't. Give my ticket to whomever you want."

Rick and I were headed for the ski slopes of Sugarbush. A friend of his owned a Bed & Breakfast in Vermont. Rick bartered personal training sessions for a long weekend, and chose to share it with me.

He was quite the wheeler-dealer. I thought I was impressed with how Kevin used to negotiate on Wall Street, but he didn't hold a candle to my Ricky. When did getting someone to make you sweat and put you through the wringer physically become negotiating currency?

"You're not coming for my birthday afternoon that you planned? And since when do you ski?" my mother shrieked into the phone.

Rick had rented a sports car and we drove there like Cary Grant and Audrey Hepburn in some old movie I once saw. We sang, badly, to the radio and left the city, as well as our lives in it, far behind us.

We checked in, and the first thing we did when we entered our quaint home away from home was to make love in the all-consuming four-poster bed. I loved being naked around him because I knew he really appreciated it; like I was a work of art. I looked at him with gratitude because he had been my sculptor.

The next day, we got up early and went down to have a hearty breakfast before we hit the slopes. Rick ordered for both of us. "Two bowls of oatmeal with bananas and apples, plus two orange juices please." We sat and bulked up on fruit and fiber so we would have plenty of energy to burn. We sat smirking at each other because we felt superior to the other guests who were gorging on piles of pancakes, doused in maple syrup; mounds of eggs and bacon and white toast smothered in butter, powered French toast also drowned in syrup with hash browns thrown on the plate for good measure. The sight of people stuffing that food in their mouths and licking sticky syrup off their fingers and smacking powder from their lips was revolting to say the least.

Later, on the ski lift, I looked back to see a portly man on line for the lift. He wore a huge white parka and matching snow pants. I remembered him from the dining room, dragging a glazed donut through the whipped cream of his hot chocolate.

"Hope we reach the mountain before the 'Ab-dom-inal Snowman' gets on," I cracked.

Rick enjoyed the joke at the guy's expense. He was the one who had pointed out the donut drag in the first place and made the comparison between a donut and a tire, and how the former created the latter around people's middles. "You're terrible," he said. "Funny, but terrible."

"Hey, it's my kid's third birthday. We're havin' a barbecue bash. Barney is making a personal appearance. You in?"

Rick and I were snuggling around a roaring fire in the Berkshires when Lisa left her message on my machine. He had bartered extra sessions for a wilderness weekend in a cabin owned by a favorite client of his.

"You? Camping? Since when?" was the most Lisa could muster through her anger when I gave her my excuse for why I didn't call back or show up.

People had pretty much given up on me by the time Rick and I had decided to go trekking up in the Adirondacks.

"If they could see me now," I sang, using jazz hands as I power walked down the trail.

"So you never exercised at all?" Rick asked incredulously.

"Years ago, I had this tape called "Eight-Minute Abs." I was too lazy to get off the couch and put the tape in the VCR, let alone do the eight-minute workout. I used to hang clothes on my exercise bike's handles. Sometimes, though, I did do leg lifts while I laid on the sofa and ate Rocky Road. I told myself I was also exercising my spoon-holding arm."

Rick laughed at my self-depreciation and at what I knew he thought was hyperbole. I let him think.

I'd become a full-blown outdoor-type girl by the time Rick and I went scuba diving on our Caribbean vacation. That trip was practically free because he bartered sessions for a week in a timeshare owned by an old pal from Wisconsin who now lived in Manhattan.

"And now here I am, doing this." I pointed to my Self-Contained Underwater Breathing Apparatus, "...in a bikini no less."

I was feeling goddess-like – standing tall, looking golden, showing off my abs, quads and glutes – until three, absolutely naturally beautiful, teenage girls in pastel, crocheted, thong bikinis walked by. They could have shamed even the most famed *Sports Illustrated* covergirls.

I made a subtle move to grab for my black on white flowered sarong. I couldn't cover myself fast enough. Even though I had an enviable torso, curvy legs and toned arms, those young girls made me feel old. Oh great. Now I had a new thing to worry about. Was there an exercise that could turn back time, I wondered.

Then as suddenly as insecurity had come upon me, it dissipated. My haughtiness came raging back when Rick observed, "You know, to the untrained eye they probably look like models, but they are flab waiting to happen. They should really tone up."

That man always knew the right thing to say.

I nodded my head in agreement, looked at the hot young things with new eyes, and then shook my head at the "stupid" girls, who didn't know enough to jog the beach, as Rick and I would do after our underwater adventure.

That evening in the hotel, I slid out of bed after he was asleep from our most ferocious night of passion ever, and, by the Aruba moonlight, admired my naked, flawless body in the blond oak armoire's full-length mirror.

# Chapter 17

## "Heavy Hitter"

The following Monday morning, tanned as well as toned, I returned to work and presented to the *TREND* client in my official role as VP and Supervisor. Since the final touches of the presentation were done in my absence, I basically read from the brief my staff had prepared. As I pontificated, I took off my spring floral jacket to reveal my slender, as well as sinewy, golden frame; then I sashayed around the room like a pinup.

I remember a horrified Byron making eye contact through the glass conference room wall with Lisa. She had walked by and witnessed my *poseur* performance from the hallway.

I thought, "They're just jealous of my new success. Mental note: make new friends."

Later, when I entered Lisa's office, she was at her desk eating lunch (greasy burger, greasier fries and a diet Coke as though that would eclipse the calories of the food) while she read over the Hanes media plan.

I needed to share my *TREND* victory and decided to forgive her for the disapproving look she threw to Byron during my meeting.

"I'm amazing," I announced.

"And I'm busy," she answered without even looking up from her paperwork or burger deluxe in the always appetizing aluminum tin.

Oblivious, I continued, "No, I'm not kidding, I'm amazing. I know I'll get bumped up to SVP for this one."

"I'm not kidding either. I said I'm busy. Why don't you go tell one of your gym friends."

Jealous. Jealous. Jealous.

"Maybe I will."

Kim and I had found our comfort zone in the superficial models/movie stars/what-size-is-worn-by-whom conversation cosmos. But since my success that a.m. was in the presence of a world famous editor-in-chief who knows models/movie stars/what-size-is-worn-by-whom, I'm sure Kim would have listened attentively.

"You know, you've got, like two days worth of POINTS on that dish."

Lisa held up her blue Bic pen, "This has a point too; and you know where you can shove it."

"Oh, really. Well, if you're referring to my ass, I mean my heart-shaped tight-as-drum ass, all I can say is, you'll never have one if you keep eating three portions at a sitting."

Lisa took in a deep breath and let it out with, "Look, no one's ever gonna drool when I step on the beach. *Page Six* is never gonna care where I ate dinner last night, and..." she continued as she held up her arm and poked at the upper part making it jiggle, "...see, my Grandma Suki's body snatched me, but I could give a shit. I have a man who loves me, a baby girl I cherish and a good job. To me, that's a model life."

"Fine, you can settle for…"

"Set...Settle? Get out."

Well, since she was getting all crazy…I turned on the heels of my Jimmy Choo's and left. She could take her bad mood out on someone else.

Then I heard her Bic pen hit the hallway wall.

By the time I got to my office, there were rumblings from colleagues like, "What's going on?" "Who's yelling?" "Did someone just throw something out of their office?"

But I paid no mind. I was too preoccupied with my own mumbling, "What the hell is her problem?"

The next thing I knew, Sarah, the little assistant that could, was knocking and entering.

"Excuse me, Trish. Hi, I'm..."

"I know who you are," I said with an exasperated sigh. I knew it was wrong to take my annoyance out on her, so I tried to pull myself together and be as professional as I could possibly be. "What is it, Sarah?"

"I've been trying to get an appointment with you for months – to observe your account, but..."

"There are plenty of accounts to assist on, Sarah. You don't… "

"Oh, yeah, I know that. Actually, I've already assisted on them all and Craig said… "

*Craig says. Craig wants. Craig needs.*

"I'll give it to you straight, Sarah. You're not right for this account so you might as well not even put it on your 'to do' list."

"Actually, the summer between junior and senior year at Duke, I did an internship at *Ladies Home Journal*, so I'm familiar with the magazine industry."

*Was this girl really equating a book full of recipes and tips on how to get a stain out of a white blouse with the glamour and glory of TREND*?

"Right. I don't mean you couldn't do the work...I hear you're a very smart girl. It's just that, part of the job...the agency's job...is making the client feel comfortable. People feel comfortable when they're dealing with people who are just like themselves."

Sarah was nodding and hanging on my every word. There was something so genuine about her. You could just tell that she was one of those people who knew her paycheck wasn't a gift. She was there to work, to get the job done whatever it took. I would have liked to help her, but...

"You want me to be like the client," repeated the young woman making sure that she had comprehended.

"Right. But sometimes that's easier said than done."

"Well, how can I be like people I've never met? Oh, wait, you want me to tell you, like, my interests and stuff and if, say I play tennis and one of the clients plays tennis then we'll have that in common to talk about?"

*Dear Christ. You went to Duke? Get the hint.*

"Sort of. But it's like, not just one person; it's the client in general. For example, they're in fashion. They live it. They breathe it. They get orgasmic over a designer belt. They get apoplectic if someone even suggests they wear last season's headband. So it stands to reason that people who are so conscious of wardrobe choices want to be around others who are as well." I then gestured to myself in my sample sale Michael Kors pants, Kate Spade shoes, and Prada blouse bought at the designer consignment store, Encore, on Madison and 84th. Sarah fingered self-consciously her blue Peter Pan collar blouse. *Did she have one in every color?*

"Oh."

I was gesticulating wildly as I explained, "They work with world-famous models and respected designers and the hottest photographers. They like to talk about hair and make-up...."

Sarah caught her minimally made up corn-fed face and pony-tailed mousy brown hair in the *TREND* promotional mirror that held a place of honor on my desk. She turned away quickly from her reflection.

"Now do you know what I mean?" I asked, trying not to sound as condescending as I felt entitled to be.

An embarrassed Sarah got up to make her escape.

"Yes. I think I do. Um...I need to see Lisa, before she leaves. Excuse me and thank you for your hel... um... insights."

I suddenly had a bout of conscience. I remembered that once, I too, couldn't work on *TREND* because I didn't look as though I could be in the magazine.

"Wait."

Sarah stopped but didn't fully turn around because she was starting to tear up. I could tell because she was sniffling and using her fingers, in lieu of an absent tissue, to wipe her nostrils.

"If you show me you really are willing to do what it takes to be on the *TREND* team, I'll give you a shot. Have you ever thought about Weight Watchers?"

Sarah turned to look at me. I knew she didn't have it in her to say, "What the fuck did you just say?" but her face betrayed that that's what she was thinking. But as I said, she was there to work, to get the job done, whatever it took.

Sarah reconfigured the look on her face to reveal that she was considering her prospective boss's challenging suggestion.

When I arrived back from lunch there was a single red rose and a handwritten note on my desk. *Congratulations. See me, Craig.* What a lovely gesture, and even though I knew he hadn't actually fetched the flower or scripted the note, I was touched. Darlene, Craig's secretary/slave, had bought it, written it and left it for me as she always did with his professional as well as personal thoughtfulness. His wife's birthday and their anniversary were always remembered; his son always received a check to pay for college life incidentals; his mistress was never left out in the cold, even when he was canceling. Darlene always made sure she had a nice, colorful bouquet to accompany the conciliatory piece of bling.

I went to his office, and as he finished up on the phone – not rushing on my account – he signaled me to have a seat on the sofa. As I made my way over to the very inviting, cushy and multi-pillowed black and white printed couch, I got sidetracked by some new photos on his credenza. They were all of Craig with celebrities like Sharon Stone and Elizabeth Taylor at some fundraiser to save the world, or children of the world, or children of the world with AIDS. Although he authorized it, I'm sure it was Darlene who actually wrote out the generous check. Past the celebs, there were the obligatory shots with noted politicians – a new one of Craig with Mayor Bloomberg, one with Hillary (Bill in the background) and the must-have shot with many a Commander in Chief, where The Silver Fox is looking concerned and ready to counsel the president on world affairs. *Craig wants, Craig needs, Craig says.*

Even though this was an impressive gallery of star-studded photography, it seemed so forced. Did he really know these people? Or was this his fifteen seconds of fame? Everybody smile on three. Then he would never, ever see them again. And while they were shaking his hands and smiling, were they thinking, "Who's this guy? Advertising? What? Take the damn picture already."

Then of course, there was the family corner. Picture after picture of him and his wife with their son vacationing in what seemed to be every corner of the globe; he and Mrs. Silver Fox, in tuxes and evening gowns, respectively, at galas and balls and dinner dances. Oh my.

I always had wondered how he did all this socializing and still managed to be such a hands-on leader at our, I mean his, highly successful agency. I once questioned Darlene about this, as she was knower of all things Silver.

An eighteen-year-old Dar, as Craig and only Craig called her, had been at Ted Bates only two months when Silver staged his walk out. *A la* Renée Zellweger in *Jerry Maguire*, she walked with him, into the unknown, with the hope of becoming the right hand of this ad legend shoo-in. Her dream had come true. This was actually the only job she had ever really had and planned on keeping it until she retired or died, whichever came first.

Darlene was a diminutive woman just on the other side of fifty. Her dyed, golden-blonde hair, short delicate nails and keep-me-looking-dewy makeup were always coifed, buffed and perfectly done. She reflected well upon the man whose image was Image. Darlene actually reminded me of my Aunt Emma: sophisticated, gracious, and always keeping a respectable distance emotionally.

She who sat at the right hand of the Father was smart enough to know not to divulge any real secrets of personal or professional successes (failures were not acknowledged), but savvy enough to understand that throwing us an informational bone (even a tiny, innocuous one) every now and then would let us think we were "in" with her and in turn, share any info we came upon with her.

And so Darlene confided how Craig worked full steam ahead all day; then had the energy to party all night. In a hushed, just-between-you-me-and-the-lamppost tone, she revealed with a hint of sarcasm, the secret of the rich and social. "Well, they go. Walk in and have their photo taken. Do one lap around the room to be seen. Then leave. They can go to two, maybe three of these benefit things in one night and still be home and in bed by the eleven o'clock news."

I stood there still waiting for him to get off his call, wondering if the family shots followed the same strategy: check-in to hotel, take the "aren't we close?" family portrait for the holiday card, go separate ways for subsequent two weeks.

Photo-op walls, even this one, couldn't help but let me think of my mom's picture "shrine" to my father. Not a forced shot in the bunch. Dear God, in every photo he looked like a towering movie star; Sam Malone, before anyone created the character for *Cheers*, with jet black hair, straight white teeth, an easy, natural, Ultrabrite smile, twinkling eyes, and always an arm around a lucky someone. Most the time it was my mother or me, but there were lots of candid shots with him and buddies – fishing, playing cards, sitting on our stoop shooting the breeze with neighbors. Everyone loved him. When my dad needed or wanted or said, they gladly obliged because people like to help those they genuinely like.

I came out of my trance when I heard the phone click, and turned to see Craig approaching me with arms out stretched. For a moment I panicked. Was he going to hug me? Ew. Would I let him? I just couldn't. There was only so much I was going to do for my job. How was I going to get out of this one? From ten feet away we could all smell his bathed on Ralph Lauren Polo for Men and come away with a minor sinus headache. From an inch away though, I just might've passed out.

But the problem never materialized. “I’m so proud of you,” he said as he took my hands, lifted my arms so they were outstretched then took a step back to have a good look at me.

In that moment, I had a flashback to my father who used to do that all the time, whether my accomplishment had been to win the lead in the school play or simply help my mother with the dishes. He always found a reason to be proud and compliment me. He always took a step back as though he had to see all of me. He didn’t want to miss a thing.

When he was taken from us, I thought the only way to cope was to not think about how much I missed him. Without him to fill me up with love and affection, I of course turned to food as my sustenance. But those days could be behind me now. I could never replace my father, but maybe I would finally have a father figure to give me what I’d been deprived of for so long: supportive male attention.

Craig smiled and continued with, “You are my new little money maker.”

Well, so much for that.

“You,” he said, “are going to keep my highest profile client happy and help me bring in even more business. A double threat: You’re smart and, well, you’ve become quite the looker again,” harkening back to when I first started working there. “And who doesn’t want to buy something from someone who looks so, well, good selling it?”

Even though his idiotic, sexist remark could have so easily been spun into a seven-figure sexual harassment suit, I smiled. I don't even know why. I guess because I was at a loss for words. I mean he was complimentary – he did call me smart after all, so he knew I wasn't an empty designer suit, like Chelsea – but still I couldn't help but feel insulted at the same time. Or maybe I was just let down that I was still fatherless and didn't have the energy to object to Craig's idea of encouragement.

"Now, let's talk about your raise."

Let's.

And we did.

I left his office, fully believing in the axiom that you can never be too rich or too thin.

## Chapter 18

### "Weigh This"

I jumped from one success to the next, as the following day I headed for Weight Watchers. It was time for my monthly weigh-in.

I loved going to my weigh-ins. Counselors and dieters alike praised me, fawned over me, and saw me as a role model who gave hope to those just embarking on their weight loss journey. The person who ran the meeting kept asking me if I wanted to become a counselor. "Oh, if I only had the time," I would gush.

As usual, I was certainly pleased with the number the official Weight Watchers scale had declared. It felt as though they were announcing the winning lotto numbers.

As I stepped off the scale, a counselor signaled me over; I thought to congratulate me as well as implore me once again to become a mentor.

"What's up?" I said, so self-satisfied that if I had been an onlooker, I would have started hating me.

"Um. You're weight is down... a lot."

"I know, I've never felt so good about myself." I unconsciously punctuated the word "good" by rolling up on the balls of my feet, then down again with a slight shoulder shrug like a kid awaiting her first prize medal at the swim meet.

She, I believe, consciously rolled her eyes and took a deep breath in an effort to let me know how tedious she found me. Then she began to address me as though she were a teacher speaking to a remedial student who didn't understand that "F" doesn't stand for "Fine."

"Right and that's great. It's also obvious," she continued as she eyeballed my wanna-see-me-bench-press biceps, "that you exercise, which we also emphasize be done in, um, moderation. It's wonderful to feel a sense of accomplishment. That's what keeps us "with the program" as they say. But what I'm trying to bring out is that your weight's not only down, but it's under the healthy range for your frame and, let's see," she said checking the DOB on my file, "you're in your late twenties, early thirties?"

"What? I've never been healthier."

"Well, yeah you have. Look, here's the chart." She whipped out this "very official" looking thing with columns for height, age, whatever and then the corresponding weight the Department of Health or the Weight Watchers gods deem appropriate. Apparently I was the perfect weight if I had been four inches shorter and sixteen-years-old.

"See. For your height and age, your weight should be in this range and you're roughly fifteen pounds under that. So, we want you to increase your intake by ten POINTS a day then..."

"Then you can make me fat again."

"Please calm down. No one at Weight Watchers wants to see you or anyone destroy their progress or success, let alone "be fat." However, we feel there is an obligation on our part to tell you when you weigh too little and help guide you into a weight range that's healthy."

Her tone had transitioned from condescending to that of a nurse on television when the scene calls for her to talk down a mental patient, *No one's going to hurt you. We're all your friends here.* Then a syringe-wielding colleague sticks the patient with a long needle. When the sedative kicks in, she lets out a shrill, *Quick, we need a psych consult down in the ER.*

"I came here so you people could help me lose weight and now that I've lost it you want me to gain it back so then I'll have to start coming back once a week again, so you can make more money off me. I'm in advertising. I know a marketing ploy when I see one. I'm sure you also have an obligation to meet a certain quota with corporate. Well, not off me. I don't think so."

I started to stomp away from this shape saboteur.

"Wait. Excuse me. Excuuuuuuuuse me." She was as pissed as I was. When I did not heed her command, she started to hurry after me. "I said excuse me. Please wait a minute." As I by-passed the elevators and swung open the door to the stairwell, she stopped, but kept shouting from the middle of the hallway. "It's my job to help you manage your weight. If I see someone fall into an unhealthy range, I am obliged to..." The two-ton stairwell door slammed shut and cut off her retributions.

I pushed past some familiar faces; other members who took the stairs for exercise. They stared and looked a little scared as I yelled over my shoulder, "I don't need your help. I don't need this place anymore either."

I pushed open the door to the street with such force that for a moment I feared the glass would break. When it didn't, I got my bravado back and power walked through crowded Greenwich Village. Everyone – at Weight Watchers, in the Village, no, make that all of lower Manhattan, no, all of Manhattan, and especially those at Image – could eat my dust, and I hoped it had lots of POINTS.

## Chapter 19

### "Down-sizing"

I capped off my morning with those who were trying to fatten me up by spending my afternoon with someone who, I was positive, was trying to drag me down into the bowels of insanity.

"And so," I told my mother, "Chelsea just couldn't cut it. I mean even if she hadn't gotten sick, she just didn't have the smarts. Craig says that I'm the whole package – looks and brains – and I'm going to be his new-business pitch woman because people want to buy what I'm selling."

I was talking so loudly that other Bloomingdale's shoppers were looking at me – then each other – like, *Who is that self-important bitch?*

My mother, though, was beaming. "I'm so happy for you. You were always a smart girl. You just didn't always take care of yourself. Now that you are, everything is coming together. I want to buy you something nice for the business trip so you can be impressive in front of Julia Roberts."

My mother had always been generous. Always rewarded my accomplishments. I think, however, this was the first time she had ever done so without using an edible substance as the trophy.

"Here, these are cute," said my mother as she held up a pair of Lily Pulitzer capris in black with a bright yellow, pink and blue palm tree print. They would be great for the Miami leg of the *TREND* shoot.

"OK, I'll try them. What size you got?"

"Two."

"I'm a zero, now. I'm pretty sure."

"I can't believe that they make clothes in size zero. It sounds so silly. But," she said examining the pants, "these look awfully small. Why don't you just try them?"

"Because they're not my size. Can you not count? Zero," I shrieked, drawing a letter "Z" in the air with my index finger as though I had channeled Zorro.

She went from proud to exasperated and just wanted me to shut up. People were once again staring. "Fine. I'm sorry I showed them to you."

We were now arguing over a circular chrome clothing rack.

"Well, honestly Mother, you're so insulting," I tried to explain, hoping finally she would understand me.

"I'm what?"

"Offering someone something a size bigger than they wear is insulting," I said as I grabbed the Lily's in the smallest size, turned and started to click-clack away.

"I liked you better when you were fat," I could have sworn I heard my mother mumble under her breath.

I spun around on my kitten heels so fast that I almost landed on my ass right in front of the promotional model assaulting people with spritzes of Dior's *J'Adore*.

"What?"

My mother grabbed quickly for a coordinating Lilly Pulitzer bright yellow top that happened to be on a nearby rack and said, "Sweater to go with that?"

That evening, after Rick and I finished my workout, he kissed me goodbye and went to greet his next client. What a relief it was to not only have a way to release the stresses of the day, but to be with someone who supported all my effort to maintain my figure.

I cleaned up and decided to wait at the health bar until he finished his appointments. While I waited for the counter guy to create my salad, I ran into a visibly bony Kim in a blue Buff Lycra tank that was big, not on purpose, and baggy Seven jeans that were designed to be skin tight.

I skipped hello, and went right for, "What size are those pants?"

"Hi to you, too."

"No seriously."

"Zero."

"Well, I just bought a zero and..."

"You're a zero now, too?"

"Yeah, and mine fit. Yours are...well, they're big?"

"Isn't it great?" Kim beamed.

"Um...I never realized you'd gotten so..."

"This is the thinnest I've ever been in my life. I'm so happy."

"OK. Um. My dinner's ready. Why don't you eat with me?"

"Sure."

I paid for my salad and Kim got a sparkling water.

I couldn't bear to hear about who was on the cover of *People*, what they were wearing or whether Kim thought she was thinner than Paris, Nicole, Lindsay or the Olsens. I started to make conversation that I actually thought would hold her attention.

"So my *TREND* pitch went great and we're going to do this campaign that's sort of a 'Behind-the-pages-of-the magazine' thing."

"You know, you never took me to any *TREND* parties like you promised."

"I haven't been to any. When I'm not here working out, I'm, well, working."

"Oh." She then became distracted by her bottled beverage. "I hope the bubbles in this don't make me fat, like bloat me or something?"

Honest to God, this girl had the attention span of a five-year-old. She was then swatting the bubbles with her straw, I presumed so she could destroy these potential bloat menaces. The Weight Watchers counselor, my mother, Kim, not to mention Lisa; I just wanted to get away from all these people who were just so aggravating to be around.

I tried to remain composed and not sound too condescending when I remarked, "Right. I don't think anyone ever got fat from drinking water, sparkling or otherwise. So anyway, I'll be documenting every phase of putting the magazine together. I'll be traveling a lot. We're starting in South Beach to shoot the photographer who's shooting the models for the fashion spread; then ending in New Mexico to shoot the reporter and fashion photographer interviewing Julia Roberts. I'll probably be gone for a couple months – you know, the entire summer.

Kim seemed restless and preoccupied.

"Hello?" I said as I snapped my sinewy fingers in her face.

She looked at me like a petulant tenth grader who'd just been accused of not paying attention by the nagging nun. Twice in the same day, someone was rolling her eyes at me and sighing in exasperation.

"Yeah, I heard you. Documenting the magazine and you'll be traveling. That's great. Hanging with models and Julia Roberts. Really glamourous. Ask her how she lost the baby weight."

It was time to change the subject before I smacked her. "Uh-huh. You know this salad is really delicious. You want some?"

"Um...no thanks." She graciously left off the words, "You asshole," from her refusal.

I ignored her and put some on my fork and offered it to her like a mother trying to get her toddler to eat peas. I hoped that I would not have to resort to making airplane noises and asking her to, "Open the hangar."

"Here. Just have a little. I'm telling you, it's really good. Have you eaten today?"

Kim grew pale as she eyed the forkful of food. For a minute there I thought she was going to throw up. "Is that...an ar...ti...choke?" Then her face went from ashen to anger red. "That's an artichoke. You know how many calories are in artichokes?"

I looked around, like a cop searching for back-up.

"Calm down," I said. Now I was sounding like one of those TV nurses.

"You're trying to make me fat," she yelled.

I pushed my chair back from the table so I could make a run for it, just in case she tried to attack me with my evil artichoke-loaded fork.

"Again with this?" I said more annoyed then I wanted anyone to see.

Offering someone a bite of a vegetable is not interfering with someone's diet. Now, those Weight Watchers people trying to get me to raise my POINTS count as to gain weight, well, that was undermining. But a forkful of salad? Oh c'mon.

"You see how hard I work at being 'Slim Kim' and you try to feed me an artichoke? Some friend!"

Kim got up with such force she turned over the table accidentally and stormed away without remorse. The clean freak Buff maintenance people came running to erase any trace of Slim Kim's heavy scene. Other Buff patrons watched in confusion. I just shook my head in disbelief.

Rick to the rescue. "What was that?" he said as he came running over.

"Oh, who knows?" I was totally fed up – with everything. I just wanted to get away. "I'll wait 'til I get back to talk to her."

## Chapter 20

### "That's Big of You"

Lisa walked into my office for what looked like a civilized showdown. For as long as I'd known her, she had always been one of those people who liked to clear the air, and then move on.

"We need to talk," she said straight-faced and monotone.

"I know," I said, mirroring her look and sound. I really did know and I really did want to stop being in "a thing" with her. I loved this woman. She was my friend, the Stiller to my Meara, but I was just so fried that I wished we could have put it on hold for now.

As Lisa was about to close the door, Sarah the Assistant as she was now called, popped in wearing her attempt at fashionable clothes and more makeup.

"Sorry to interrupt," she said to a speechless Lisa. Sarah the Assistant then turned to me with a look that said, "How do I look?" as she was saying, "Am I *TREND* yet?"

I had seen pastel-dyed Easter eggs that were subtler than her eye shadow choices. She was wearing some pink leopard sack dress monstrosity that she probably found strewn on an "As-Is" table at Filene's Basement. Her costume reminded me of what Grandma Clown was wearing when I took Lisa's daughter to The Big Apple Circus. Just to get rid of her, I winked and assured her, “Gettin’ there. The lipstick’s a little last season, but good try.”

Sarah the Assistant looked as though she was making a mental note, then gave me a thumbs-up and left.

I rolled my eyes to Lisa, who closed the door with a slight slam. So much for the “civilized” part of the showdown.

“What was that?” she demanded.

“Sarah’s trying to make herself *TREND*-worthy.” I pointed to some of the covers that adorned my corked wall. Then I snickered, “Good luck.”

“*TREND*-worthy?” She said this as though the notion that there were people in the world who shouldn’t even be allowed to turn the pages of the magazine with their unmanicured fingers was unheard of.

“Look, what can I say? The magazine isn’t for everyone and not just anyone can work there. So not just anyone can work on it here.”

Lisa’s mouth was so wide open I could see the dental work it took her every Wednesday for six months to complete.

“I gave Sarah a chance to rise to the occasion so she could help out on *TREND*, but as you could see…” I trailed off gesturing to the recently shut door and finished with a shrug; both arms bent at the elbow and my palms up.

Lisa took a big breath in. So big, you could see her chest expanding with air. I knew this move too well. Right as she felt her anger going up her spine at Mach 5, and felt her head ready to blow off, she would reach deep inside herself to find composure. Upon letting the air out, she was always able to speak in a calm, slow monotone that bordered on a little scary.

"OK. How can I put this?" God she was predictable. "When you lost your big. Fat. Ass. Where your brain was obviously housed, you also must have... lost your mind!" She yelled that last part so loud I was contemplating calling security. So much for predictable. I had never heard her raise her voice before. This was even scarier than the slow, modulated serial-killer tone.

I decided to not fight fire with fire, first, because I was mentally exhausted, second because since things were going so well for me, I could afford to take the high road.

"OK, I know where this is coming from," I interrupted with a wave of my hand.

She ignored me and kept going, "...as well as your character. Your compassion. Your dignity. Your..."

"You're jealous," I re-interrupted.

Well, that shut her up, if only momentarily.

"C-c-come again?" She stammered, looking truly flabbergasted, like someone who can't balance a checkbook being asked to decipher a calculus problem in her head.

"I've been waiting for this," I continued matter-of-factly. "I'm working on a higher profile account than you..."

"You're delusional." Now she looked scared.

"Hence I am becoming more high profile than you..."

She was shaking her head and starting to hyperventilate. "Have you had enough POINTS today? Feeling light-headed?"

I smirked at her sarcasm. She was losing it. I was winning. "Then, I'm sure you heard about my raise."

Lisa rolled her eyes now. "Everybody gets a raise when they sell a major campaign. I got one too."

Ignoring her, I continued, "And frankly, I just look better than you - and you can't stand it anymore."

Her face went blank. Our talk had mentally and physically drained her of all emotion. She was over me. "Honey, it's you I cannot stand." She opened the door to leave.

"And now with my trip and shoot with supermodels and Julia..." I was still going as though she had not said anything.

She gave me the so-what eye roll. "I'm shooting, too."

"You are?" I said confusedly.

"I'm shooting a new Hanes campaign. With celebrities." She stopped short of sticking her tongue out at me.

"Well, we never got to talk about that because you kicked me out of your office after my big meeting." See it was all her fault.

"Yeah, I meant to ask. What was with the pin-up prance in the meeting? You used to make fun of Chelsea when she did it."

"I criticized her because I was jealous of her." There. See, there's a big person in this perfect package, admitting my character defect. "That's why I'm not mad at you for what you're saying. As I said, I understand where you're coming from."

"Good. OK." The predictable controlled monotone was back. "And understand where I'm going – out of this office and as far from you as possible."

She was not getting the last word. I got up, walked around my desk and stood in the door jam. "Well," I yelled after her as she marched down the hall, "that'll be easy, since I'm leaving for Florida."

From inside her office she shouted, "Don't send a postcard."

I just shook my head in pity at my poor resentful former friend as I watched heads pop out of their offices to see what all the ruckus was about.

Days later, all my stresses gave way to excitement as I got ready for my trip. I tried to pack, but Rick kept sidetracking me with kisses.

"This is such a big deal for me," I shared.

"I'm happy for you. I'll miss you, but I'm happy you're doing well."

He playfully unpacked what he considered "too sexy" underwear.

"These will be staying home."

"Hey, what if I meet a male model who wants to know my Victoria's Secret?" I joked.

He threw me on to the bed to tickle me as he started to remove the VS lacy white bra and matching panties I currently had on.

"Then you tell him, that's Rick's secret."

I loved being loved.

The next day I, and my new Polo Ralph Lauren luggage, was in the office tying up loose ends before it was time to take off.

Byron, in a straw Fedora, white linen pants and jacket, white silk t-shirt and brown leather Prada sandals came by to pick me up – luggage-free of course. The only thing he planned to carry were his Oliver Peoples tortoiseshell shades. He had Fedex-ed his luggage (a trick he learned from one of the *TREND* editors) so it would be waiting for him at the hotel when he arrived; leaving him unencumbered and able to walk around Teterboro like he not only owned the private plane, but the airport as well.

I had no problem schlepping because I wanted everyone to know I was a world traveler, and my world was currently New York-Miami-Paris-Australia-L.A.-New Mexico and back.

"Come on Miss Thing, the limo awaits," Byron said as though to the manner born. "You don't want to miss the plane."

"You mean 'corporate jet'," correcting him so he would remember that I knew where he really had been born. I then tried to hand him a small carry-on satchel so I would not have to juggle it with my handbag, make-up case and valise. "Here, take one of these."

"You're kidding me, right? Do I look like a Sky Cap to you? I sent mine ahead so I wouldn't have to schlep, Miss Trish."

And people think editors and supermodels are divas.

I dropped all pretenses and tossed my Chanel sunglasses on my desk, so we could talk Bronx to Queens. "You can't carry one friggin' bag just down the elevator to the car? Here, I'm giving you the satchel. I'm taking the suitcase and make-up carryall for God's sake."

He sighed and snatched the bag out of my hand and snapped, "Dang, girl. Let's just go."

Well, we were getting off to a great start.

As we headed down the hall, Byron and I passed Lisa going back into her office with what used to be one of our favorite lunches to share: a Subway sandwich. We used to get the foot long and split it. For a moment I wondered whether it was the turkey, provolone, lettuce, green peppers and black olives with lite mayo and a splash of oil and vinegar on the hearty Italian cheese and herb bread or the meatball parmigiano hero. I know those ads say that guy lost weight eating Subway, but it never worked for us. When I think of what I used to shove in my mouth, well, perhaps it's best Lisa and I are no longer friends.

"Good trip, Byron," she said to him as she looked at me.

Fine. I would ignore her too.

Byron waved his hand like George Clooney shooing at the paparazzi, and gave Lisa a don't-put-me-in-the-middle-of-this look; then we got on the elevator.

Just as the doors were about to close, an even more done up Sarah the Assistant flagged me down from the middle of the hallway.

"I joined Weight Watchers," she hollered as she held up a Weight Watchers Snack Bar. "Only two POINTS."

In my peripheral vision, I could see a totally unnerved Byron staring at me.

The doors closed across my face as I nodded to Sarah and smiled a God-help-us-all smile.

I then turned to Byron. "Don't ask."

# Chapter 21

## "Slim to None"

Having spent all of the summer away from the sticky and often stinky city, I returned refreshed and welcomed the New York Fall. I was now a corporate jet-setting crony of supermodels and semi-houseguest of superstar, Julia Roberts.

I had been vague with Rick about my exact return date because I wanted to surprise him as he had surprised me in Miami.

We had landed at Teterboro late Friday night. After a good sleep, I headed to the gym that Saturday afternoon, walking into Buff and waving at the receptionist as though she were a long lost friend.

She greeted me with the phrase I so rightly had earned, "Hey stranger, you're looking buffalicious."

Being away, even though work is work no matter where you do it, had been a nice break for me. Even with my number-fifty sunscreen and wide brimmed hat, I had gotten a nice healthy glow, sweetened by my Clarins self-tanner.

"And feeling buffalicious I might add. Just stopping by to see Rick."

"Not here. He took off," she chirped.

I stopped in my tracks. "Oh. Um...OK." I looked around and saw The Bombshells and many of the other gym "residents," who by this time, I was sure didn't have apartments because they figured that their gym membership fee was cheaper than rent, so they just camped out. But someone was nowhere in sight.

"Before I go, have you seen Kim?" I was hoping she'd be in better spirits than when I left; also a little less skeletal. I was actually excited about sharing all the supermodel news, and to tell her that I had in fact asked Julia how she lost all the baby weight. Kim was the only person who would truly appreciate these stories.

The receptionist just looked at me. "Rick didn't tell you?"

"What?"

"Uh, nothing, um... he'll... "

I hate this kind of coy, game-playing bullshit.

"What already?" I said in a, I'm-the-paying-customer tone of voice.

I think I sort of scared her because she just blurted out, "Kim is gone."

"Gone where?"

I ran to Rick's Chelsea apartment – fourteen blocks north and five more to the west. Yes, I ran to West 23rd Street and Tenth Avenue in heels, forgetting all about my "street paranoia," and didn't stop for the horn-honking-crazy-cabdriver traffic.

I almost got "gone" myself a few times, but luckily the taxis stopped in time. I was bumping into people, old, young, fat, thin, some with packages, others with babies in Snugli's, and not even looking back when they yelled the New Yorker's battle cry, "Hey, excuuuuuuuuuuuse me."

When Rick, naked from the waist up, jumprope in hand and sweaty, opened the door, he found me out of breath and on the verge.

"Babe. You didn't say you'd be home toda..."

I ran in, pushing him aside, which was sort of like moving a mountain, relieved to be there, but still unable to calm down. Too frantic to ask for a paper bag, I pulled the neck of my turtleneck up over my nose and mouth and began to breath slowly and deeply. I was glad that I wore "Unscented Secret."

He watched me hyperventilate with his mouth open. When I finally had collected myself enough to speak, I pulled down my sweater/mask and stammered, "I...we...left last...I wanted to surprise... so I went to the club...then, I asked for Kim..." Then my turtleneck went back over my mouth and nose.

He closed his mouth, put down the rope and used his wristband to mop his forehead. Then, like a surgeon delivering the bad news, he took a caring yet professionally distant stance and explained, "It happened obviously when you were away. We found out when her sister came to clean out her locker."

Sister?

I yanked my sweater down with such force that I believe I heard the neck seams rip. "And you didn't tell me?"

"And I didn't tell you," he repeated in what I thought was a little too cavalier a manner, somewhat like a self-righteous adult speaking to an agitated child.

"She was my friend," I yelled. "How could you not tell me she..."

He rolled his eyes. He rolled his fucking eyes. No, I must be seeing things.

"Did you just roll your eyes?"

He tried to recover from his inappropriate gesture, by taking a calm, rational tone. "First of all, she wasn't really your friend. She was someone from the gym you just hung out with while you were waiting for..."

"What do you mean she 'wasn't really my friend'?"

Ignoring me, he continued, "Second, what were you going to do? Come back from your career-making trip? For what? To pay your respects to someone you hardly knew? I sent flowers and a sympathy card from the both of us by the way."

I guess he expected me to thank him for throwing my name on a card, like the only thing that mattered was that the dead girl's family would give me credit for being thoughtful.

I was holding both sides of my head in fear my skull was going to crack down the middle and if I didn't have a good grip at the temples then both halves would end up on the *parqué* floor.

"What are you talking about? Why are you saying she wasn't my friend? She was like a little sister." I was starting to tear up, less from the abrupt discovery of my loss, and more from the tension headache brought on by Rick's end of the conversation. He seemed to be working hard to stifle a yawn.

"What'd she do for a living?"

This popped out of his mouth so quickly that he sounded like a game show host, except he left off the part about "For $200 and the trip to Bermuda..."

"Wha... what?" With my shoulders now hitched up around my ears, I couldn't quite hear.

"That's right, what?"

I fell back in his giant cordovan leather club chair that practically hugged you when you sat in it. This time though I felt as though it were restraining me.

I was quiet now. I had such a throbbing in my head that I also couldn't think. "Um...I could swear she told me...but I...you know, I'm not sure she ever said."

"Of course she never said. All she ever said to anyone was about how she looked, or what diet she was on, or what size she was wearing..."

In my trance-like state I continued for him, "what models and actresses she was thinner than..."

Rick picked up with, "You know how many times the gym physician and counselors tried to reason with her?"

"I mean I thought she was getting too skinny...but who was I to say any..."

"I thought you said you were her friend? No wait, her big sister," rubbing in his remark with a smirk and a tone I had never heard him use.

I just looked at him. And I didn't recognize him.

"See, you weren't really close or you would have said something."

I got up and covered my mouth like I was going to throw up. I walked feebly around the room trying to get my balance. I went from chair to table to the other table to mantelpiece. It was like I was square dancing with inanimate objects.

Rick just stood there and watched, bored yet slightly amused, the way I, as a young girl, used to look at those old-world Italian relatives who'd drape themselves over the coffin at wakes.

"Look, not to speak ill of the dead, but I never liked you hangin' out with her anyway. She was crazy."

My saliva tasted like bile. "She was sick."

"Yeah, sick in the head," he snickered, as he thumbed through *Men's Workout* magazine.

"She had a disease. How can you be so insensitive?"

"Because I've been there. I was the fat kid remember? I know from bad body image."

I stopped to grab on to the hall table because I felt faint. When I looked up I was staring at my reflection in the hall mirror.

"She was so afraid of her weight." I didn't know at that moment whether I was talking about Kim or myself.

"I learned to eat right, to exercise," he continued as he flipped to the next page.

We were each having our own conversations – with ourselves.

"She thought a salad would make her fat," I mumbled.

"I have no patience for people with no self-control. That goes for people who eat too little as well as too much."

"Like people who can't control reciting the POINTS value of each donut every time they pass a Dunkin' Donuts?"

I couldn't look at myself any more. Or listen to him.

I believe he was saying something about how she would have benefited more from a psychiatrist than a weight trainer, when I opened the front door and walked, like a zombie, back down to my Greenwich Village digs.

# Chapter 22

## "Food for Thought"

I did not sleep the entire night. I spent the dark hours telling off Rick. In my mind-argument, he was humbled and silent; I was in control, and of course, right. Kim was a friend and I had cared. I believed this whole-heartedly because if you say something to the dancing shadows on your ceiling enough times, it becomes true.

After a brief and unrecuperative nap, that came about just as the streetlights were going down and the sanitation trucks were revving up, I decided to spend my Sunday gathering the evidence that would prove Rick wrong.

I hurried toward Gramercy Park checking my handwritten paper against the addresses I was passing along Irving Place. I felt like a Jehovah's Witness or Avon Lady as I stood there ringing the doorbell of a stranger.

The young woman came to the front door of the brownstone and looked through the glass panes only to see the face of someone who had clearly just seen a ghost.

"Yes?"

After she said it twice, shook her head, and was about to walk back inside, I blurted out, "I knew Kim."

She came back and opened the heavy mahogany door.

"Hi, how can I help you?"

"Hi, um, my name is… " Oh Christ, what was my name? "Trish. Trish Collins. Um...I knew Kim. I never got to pay my respects. I was out of… May I come… ."

The woman wearing Kim's face – only cherubic, healthy and rosy-cheeked – stepped aside and invited me in.

Kim's twin sister, Ali, showed me to the couch via the fireplace mantle, which displayed an array of family photos, mostly of herself and her sister.

"You were a cheerleader?"

"That's Kim. It was after we slimmed down."

I then came across a picture of the chubby twosome at ten.

"I was satisfied with the fifteen I had lost in sophomore year of high school, and just managed to keep it off – a lot less junk, and I used to play on the basketball team. Still play in the park sometimes. But Kim, she was so afraid she'd gain it back. It was one crazy diet after another," Ali explained as she went to putter in the kitchen, leaving me to explore the parts of Kim's life that I had never known existed. A svelte Kim at Halloween, dressed in some disco ensemble complete with black-spangled tube top and bright red Lycra hot pants. The shapely sisters in black strapless dresses at a wedding, Kim with the catch of the day – the bridal bouquet.

"The shot with the bathing suit. You or Kim?"

"You mean the itsy-bitsy, teeny-weeny, yellow-polka-dot bikini? That's me." Ali rolled her eyes and added, "My sister wore a one-piece because she thought she was still too fat for a two-piece."

Ali served us tea in mismatched floral cups and saucers. I declined the scones she offered. As she ate hers, all I could think was that Slim Kim would not have touched that with a ten-foot pole. Then I thought, "Fuck it," cut one of the cakes in half, and ate it with butter in loving memory of my dead pal.

"Your apartment is great," I said.

The whole place looked like something out of a Laura Ashwell Shabby Chic coffee table book.

"Thanks. Now that I live in it alone, it seems too much," she answered as I settled back in someone's grandmother's floral armchair and she on the green velvet settee.

"So," she continued in a tone that implied that it was time we got down to business, "you said you knew my sister from...?"

"The gym."

"Buff," she said, acknowledging the place that was Kim's home away from home with slight disapproval. "Right. So anyway over the past few years, as you probably know, things weren't going too well for her, and the dieting and exercising just got taken to the extreme."

"What wasn't going well?"

"You know, failing out of college. I mean she was smart enough; she was just too distracted by some glamorous life she thought she was missing out on. Then trying to get into the fashion industry, and having it not exactly turn out the way she had hoped. And of course, she must have mentioned her fiancé marrying someone else. Oh God, that was a nightmare."

"I didn't... I had a fiancé who... it's so hard when that happens," I whispered.

"So the two of you had that in common. Is that how you became friends? You shared that with her to comfort her? Let her know that that kind of thing just didn't happen to her?"

"Well, no, not exactly."

Ali stared at me and looked, well, a little uncomfortable. She sipped her tea and the silence made me even more anxious. I knew I was probably digging my own grave here, but after Rick's challenge, I had to know.

"What did she do? You know, as her job?"

Now, looking annoyed and suspicious, Ali put down her teacup firmly on the coffee table and said, "I'm sorry, I thought you said you were a friend of my sister?"

"Right," I affirmed with a very exaggerated head nod that made me look like a bobble-head doll, "at the gym. So, um, we didn't talk a lot about personal..." I started to tear up and my voice started to break, as I continued, "So anyway, her work?"

My wet eyes spared me from getting thrown out on my ass, but they did not save me from being escorted out, in only the politest of ways. Ali said we could continue our conversation as she walked her dog around Gramercy Park, "since this is his usual time to go." I knew it was a just a ploy to get the "crazy woman" out of her apartment, since the pooch looked perfectly content sitting at his owner's feet.

"Kim was a receptionist in the garment district. This crappy place that churned out cheap children's clothing," I was informed as we clip-clopped down the steps of the brownstone. "She so desperately wanted to work in fashion. Her dream was to work in some famous designer's showroom or anywhere to associate with models, you know, glamorous people."

Just then we passed a group of teenage girls with a camera, who were posing for each other, imitating stances seen in fashion magazines. Everyone wants to be a model or hang out with one or date one.

"Like the people who work at *TREND* Magazine."

"Um...yeah, like that I guess," she shrugged.

I couldn't take it anymore. I sat on a bench and began to cry. "I could have helped her. I'm so sorry...I didn't..."

This young woman, who was still in mourning for her identical sibling, had by now just about enough of me, my questions, and my Nancy Drew fact-finding bullshit in general.

Cold as ice, Ali wanted to know, "Why did you come here?" All the while trying desperately to contain herself from siccing her dog on me.

"I just wanted..." I desperately began to explain, although I had no idea what I really wanted, and was unsure what words would complete my incoherent sentence. Thank God she cut me off and finished on my behalf.

"You wanted me to tell you it wasn't your fault. I can't give that kind of absolution. I need it myself."

I had never been so ashamed and embarrassed. Ali was still deep in sorrow and obviously had her own regrets and guilt about what she did or didn't do for her sister. And I had been feeling sorry for myself? This was clearly the pinnacle of self-absorbed asshole-ness in my life thus far. Rick had been right. There had been no need to call me and tell of "my loss." I probably would have shed a few tears in the hotel suite, before meeting up with Byron for some down time shopping.

Ali would have whipped me with the dog leash if she'd known that I deigned to let Kim keep me company after workouts, company I didn't even always enjoy.

What was hitting me so hard was the realization of what I had become. Someone so obsessed with working on my outside, that I had stopped working on what's inside.

I rose, wiped my eyes and blew my nose; trying to regain what little dignity I had so that Ali's final memory of me would not be that of a blubbering pathetic mess.

Before heading in opposite directions, Ali confessed, "I tried to help her...I tried to tell her...I tried to make her eat. I sought professional help. They told me, it was her decision; she had to want to go to counseling. She didn't want to."

"You did your best. There was nothing else you could have done," I mumbled.

"Yes, there was." Ali answered. "I could have tied her up and carried her there."

# Chapter 23

## "Eating Crow"

Monday I went back to work. The bravado with which I had left the agency had been replaced by a humble reserve. Tanned, trim and somnambulant, I walked through the halls, head down, smiling weakly in place of saying hello and just nodding when asked how my trip had gone.

This suited Byron just fine. "Then Naomi said to me... So I just had to joke with Julia about..." Byron was born to be truly the center of attention.

A noticeably un-*TREND*-worthy Sarah the Assistant hurried by, head down as well. I could not blame her; I was not worth looking at, even in Marc Jacobs. I had let things with Kim go unsaid. I would not make the same mistake twice.

"Good morning, Sarah."

"Hi, Trish. Welcome back," she said to the new black with red flecks carpeting that had been installed in my absence.

"Where's the fire? Come in a second."

Her shoulders dropped and she swallowed hard, as though she would rather shovel manure than have to spend even a second alone with me. She maintained her anywhere-but-here look as she shuffled into my office.

"How are you?" I asked, hoping she could tell how genuinely sincere I was.

"I'm...I'm sorry." She whispered. I could tell that what she was about to say was difficult and scary for her, but she was mustering up her courage to give it to me straight. "I tried to do what you suggested, you know, with my weight and hair and makeup and well, everything you pointed out was wrong with me; so that when you came back from the trip I'd be..."

She was making excuses where none were necessary. I could not let a subordinate see me cry. So I took one of Lisa's deep breaths, turned down the internal thermostat to just above Ice Queen and very professionally explained, "It's fine. You're fine. I made a mistake and I apologize."

It was like she didn't even hear me. She obviously had rehearsed her speech a million times and now that the horse had left the barn... "I just couldn't... Dieting is like a full time job for me. And besides, this is how I dress. Not very fashion forward, but it's me. And makeup, well, I never really got the knack of putting it on and quite frankly, that was OK because it's always made my face feel dirty."

My turn. "I should have never..."

Just then, one of her equally as green co-workers ran by and signaled for Sarah the Assistant to *come quick*. There was some *Craig said... Craig wants... Craig needs...* emergency.

With machine gun speed, my one-time makeover project blurted out in a single breath, "I know I can't work with you, but that's OK. I've started working full time for Lisa, and I like the Hanes account. I fit in with the people, and I get free underwear." And she was off.

Anyone else might have said that last part about the underwear as a smart aleck quip, but not Sarah. She was a young woman far from home in an entry-level position who probably looked forward to working late simply for the free dinner, who really did appreciate free anything, even cotton t-shirts and briefs.

And there I had been, before I left, encouraging her to spend money on designer clothes, makeup and a "good" hairstylist. Plus, I suggested Weight Watchers. The program isn't free, and even though I thought it had been worth every penny, I was pushing her to spend money she didn't have there as well.

I reiterated, "You're fine the way your are," hoping she could still hear me as she turned the corner into the conference room, then added, "Lisa's great. Good luck."

Even though Sarah the Assistant was long gone, Lisa was right in front of me, leaning into my doorway. Apparently, she had heard the whole conversation.

"So how many POINTS in crow?" Lisa remarked, going for cheeky not snotty.

Now her, I could let see me cry.

A while later, my friend left my office calling all that had happened between us, "water under the bridge." Jerry and Anne, together again.

Still, I felt so agitated. A million thoughts were all competing, as though there was a TV inside of my head, but someone else controlled the remote and wouldn't stop flipping channels.

I began picking things up off my desk only to immediately put them down again, peeking in and under folders, and moving things around for no apparent reason. It was like I was looking for something, but I had no idea what. Maybe an answer as to how I had become this person that no one, including myself, liked any more.

The latest issue of *TREND* had been delivered with the morning mail. Although I really didn't have the patience to sit and thumb through a magazine, I was too twitchy and had to do something. I just sort of threw it open, barely scanned a couple of pages, then stopped in my tracks at an article entitled, "Big, Brainy and Beautiful," with a full-page color picture of Bessie the plus-size model staring up at me. If there was ever anyone *TREND*-worthy, it was Bessie. On the opposite page was an interview. She was promoting her new reality TV show where she made over large women and helped them change their lives *via* their attitude.

The journalist asked her if magazines should start using real women – like in the Dove campaign – instead of models, so readers would stop feeling that they didn't measure up. Ever insightful, Bessie explained, "Even if there were no job as model and no magazines to put them in, you'd still see other women at the beach looking gorgeous in a bathing suit or in a community dressing room trying on the same outfit as you and perhaps looking better in it.

"No matter who you are, you'll always find someone more attractive, smarter, richer, more talented, and yes, thinner. We really need to stop comparing ourselves. Run your own race."

Then came the kicker. "I believe in making the most of what you've got."

I didn't even have to read the rest. I could hear her words as though she had said them to me just yesterday. "And I like what I see. If you can't say that about yourself ..."

And I couldn't. I didn't like being the skinny bitch any more than I had liked being the fat chick.

Before I closed the magazine, I caught the last line of Bessie's talk with *TREND*, "... then do something about it."

Now was as good a time as any.

## Chapter 24

### "Chew on This"

The whole incident with Rick was weighing on me, no pun intended. Just as I was about to call, the phone rang and it was him, saying he had wanted to give me a couple of days to cool down. Then he graciously accepted my apology. Rick told me he was sorry as well for not being more consoling.

I did not want to rehash the past forty-eight hours. Kim, Ali, Sarah the Assistant – all went floating in the water under the bridge along with my falling out with Lisa. Instead, I regaled him with a breezy account of what I wished had been my first day back. "Craig is out, so it was peaceful enough to settle back in and I even plan to leave on time." I then suggested dinner. "I'll fix something for us."

"You cook?" Rick said, "Since when?"

"Just be at my place by at eight," I sighed with a smile, and hung up.

Truth be told, I did not cook, although from helping my mother when I was a little girl, I knew my way around a simple pasta recipe. I planned my father's favorite – lasagna. We'd have a cool crisp salad and on the way home I'd stop off at Ferrara's in Little Italy and get a few mini-pastries for dessert. I reminded myself that the beauty of Weight Watchers was that you could eat anything as long as you stayed within your daily points.

Granted, the meal was a far cry from the way Rick usually ate, but the kind of meal my family would have had, long ago and far away, when there was always more talking and laughing than eating. It would be a true celebratory feast where we'd sample a little of everything in an atmosphere of love. He would surely understand and go along at least for one night.

At around four, I called it a day so I could prepare for that night. As I walked down the hall and was about to pass the coffee room, some remarks coming from inside caused me to stop just before the entrance so I could eavesdrop.

Three young male subordinates were being young and male.

"Oh man! Did you see her butt?" said voice one.

"It's condo size," said voice two.

"All I said was the new intern was nice," whined voice three.

"Yeah, nice and fat," joked one and two in unison, as they choked on their own laughter.

My eyes started to well up. At one time, they could have been talking about me. But worse, only recently, I might have agreed with their comments and thought the young woman deserved it for not slimming down and toning up.

"Like it's so hard to hire someone who could do the job and be dateable?" number one asked.

"Listen to this, my cousin's trying to set me up with her roommate – check out the description – 'She's got a really pretty face,'" announced three.

"Oh no...," one and two offered sounding like an *a cappella* group.

"Pretty face" means the rest of her is..." started one.

My clenched jaw began to relax as I got an idea.

"...Trish," finished bachelor number three as I walked in.

"Oh, there you are. Just the people I was looking for. Cancel plans, boys, tonight you'll be pullin' an all-nighter. As you probably know, I've been away for quite a while. I want a full report on the status of all the accounts in the agency. New business, presentations, and what we've got in production. I need to be brought up to speed."

They smiled their sycophantic smiles, which hid their confusion as to why I would actually need any of that 411, then took turns saying, "I'm on it."

As I walked away I could hear, "Oh great."

"I had plans."

"What a bit....."

I popped back in. "Oh, I forgot to say on my desk in the morning. See ya." *Hate to be ya.*

# Chapter 25

## "Gaining Perspective"

Rick arrived right on time and brought me a mixed bouquet of red and yellow roses, symbolizing love and friendship.

The table was set with my grandmother's china, which I'd never used. The lasagna, which came out as perfect as anything my mother ever prepared, was ready to be served from one of Grandma's glass and silver serving trays, which I had placed in the middle of the table, along with the salad. The tray of mini-treats was on the kitchen counter with the coffee, ready to perk as soon as the timer went off, which I set for an hour from now.

"Will Henry VIII be joining us?" he queried.

I laughed at what I thought was his joke, then explained, "I just wanted us to have a nice meal. The kind I remember having...my dad used to love this."

We sat down, and in what I thought was a solicitous gesture, Rick offered to serve. We each got the perfect size-of-your-palm portion.

"How is it?" I asked, wondering why I had to fish for a compliment.

"Cheesy."

"It's my mother's secret recipe. I used mozzarella and gorgonzola."

"Did you?"

I polished off my piece in about six bites. Rick in only three.

I was still well under my daily points, since I had not had breakfast or lunch due to my depressed and anxious state; just a grande Starbucks iced tea on the way home. When I went to cut some more, he declined.

"Don't you like it?"

"It was fine. But it was enough. I'll jump rope for a half hour to work it off."

*He wanted to work it off?* Ouch.

"I wanted us to have a nice relaxing meal, a real normal meal like my fam..., to celebrate my homecoming; you know, to make up for the one that went awry."

He just sat stone-faced and as I slid the spatula under another small piece of lasagna, he said definitively, "No, thank you." So I put it on my plate.

He did help himself to plenty of salad. I joined him and that's when he loosened up again and the conversation began to flow. He wanted to hear all about my trip, and what was to come at work. I insisted on being brought up to speed on gym gossip, which could be better than high school lunch table musings.

I had not realized how time had flown until the timer on the coffee maker went off. I poured two cups and placed the dessert tray between us.

Rick looked visibly repulsed as I savored a mini-chocolate covered cannoli with a mini-cream puff chaser.

He finally picked up a pastry, I thought to eat, but instead he placed it on my plate. I was about to tell him that I had had my quota of food for the day, when he sneered, "Here, have another. In fact..." He swapped the dessert dish in front of me for the dessert tray. "Have 'em all."

Before the other day in his apartment, I had never seen him be mean. Now, I was getting an encore. Maybe I was finally seeing the real him. "What's your problem?" I demanded to know.

"If I had known you were inviting me over to watch you pig out… "

"What?"

"What's gotten into you, besides ricotta cheese and cream filling?"

If his attitude were not so abusive, I might have shared that I was tired – and not from jet lag. Tired in that existential way, when you have exhausted yourself with behavior that has not benefited you the way you'd hoped. I was burned out from a lifetime on the yo-yo, of either being so obsessed with being thin that I feared a grape would make me fat or so heavy that I was a flight of stairs away from a heart attack.

Because this time, instead of some fad diet, I had chosen a respected weight loss program, I had actually learned a lot about the role of food choices and exercise, but, of course I even took that to the extreme; hence, the Weight Watchers counselor chasing after me to tell me to put on some pounds.

I never wanted to go back to some unhealthy silhouette, but truthfully, there was no reason in the world to train like I was gearing up for the Miss Bodybuilder contest or to be size zero. It's not as though if you whittle down to the smallest size you win a prize or something; the clothes aren't cheaper just because they use less material.

There had to be a middle-weight, no, a way to live life in the middle, in a healthy place physically and emotionally. I had lived in a place like that once, along with my father and my mother. I knew I could never go back, but I really wanted to find my own version of it.

"Is this how you started eating again on your trip? If it is, I won't put up with it."

"What are you saying? If I ate a little too much... if I gained a little...? You only love me if I'm thin?"

"Yes."

"Yes?" Wow, he had more nerve than Kevin. At least Rick was honest about being a superficial jerk.

"Look, you asked." Then he smirked, "I'm sure you'd prefer that I sugar-coated it. Or if that poor excuse for a meal you served is any indication, cheese-coated it; but I don't want to be around people who can't control their food intake, Miss Second Helping. You know I've vowed to never again become what I once was. And part of keeping myself in check, is surrounding myself with people who aren't going to throw me off track."

*Cheese-coat? Second helping?* My head was pulsating. My breathing was heavy and deliberate, but I would not lose it and give myself an excuse to drown my sorrows in the remainder of my mini-friends from Ferrara's.

I remained calm, got up from the table, walked over and opened my front door. "You know, I understand exactly where you're coming from, and the last thing I want to do is throw you off track. I want to throw you out."

Or as my father had been known to say at closing time, *You don't have to go home, but you can't stay here.*

## Chapter 26

### "Sizing Things Up"

Rick, in fact, all things Buff really had to be put behind me if I was going to truly start anew. My membership at the gym was up for renewal in a couple of months anyway, so I just let it lapse. I was not ready or interested in getting involved with another health club or its members, so to keep up a fitness routine, I surfed the 'net and purchased a new stationary bike, one which cost almost as much as a gym fee and should have come with a NASA instructor to decipher all the bells and whistles.

I also decided to do something I never, ever, thought I'd do: gain weight on purpose. Yes, I was actually going to finally take the advice of my former Weight Watchers counselor, who had advised I get my weight back into the healthy range.

For the first time, I would not be packing on the pounds due to an emotional, gorge-frenzy in front of the refrigerator, eating ice cream from the carton with the freezer door open, but by increasing my daily POINTS by ten with sensible foods as the counselor had suggested – you know, before I ran from her as though she were going to hold me down and force feed me with an I.V.

Being out of the office for so long, I also lost my nine-to-five (ha! When did I ever leave at five?) groove. I really needed to get my head back in the game as we were to spend the next two weeks shooting the New York end of the "Behind-the-Scenes" campaign at the offices of *TREND,* then inside the tents at Olympus Fashion Week.

"This is the last leg of the marathon, girlfriend," said Byron, as we ascended to the penthouse floor of the Fifth Avenue building where *TREND* worked its magazine magic.

For the record, no one was scurrying through the corridors raising their voices in celebration to *Think Pink*! as I had once seen in an ancient Doris Day movie where she played an editor. The only word to describe the *TREND* team was serious – yes, even when they were talking about traffic light green being the new black. There were no *Ugly Betty*-type hijinks. No *The Devil Wears Prada* theatrics. They were there to work and they did their jobs with powdered nose-to-the-grindstone gusto.

Next came the hustle and bustle of Fashion Week – the most glamorous and scary-busy thing I had ever been exposed to in my life. Not since I attended Our Lady of Perpetual Pain and Guilt grammar school had I been screamed at so much. No one was glad to see us, nor our photographer, and did not care that we were shooting the *TREND* ad campaign. "You're in the way... get out of the way." It was not the most pleasant shoot I'd ever been on but we managed to get what we needed.

With all the heavy lifting done, Byron and I, with our subordinates, accepted the fact that for the next four weeks we would be working some very long hours culling through all the photographs and turning them into what would end up as ads in magazines, sales films, media kits, on billboards, sides of busses as well as bus and phone kiosks, plus an online effort.

Late nights equal late night dinners and absent minded eating, but with the same determination I showed when I was taking off the weight, I stayed within my new POINTS range and made sure to put in my time on my space age bike before work, as I knew I'd be too beat after.

The change in my eating and exercise routines meant that, by the time our presentation rolled around, I had put some meat back on my still slender and compact bones.

I went to Craig's office to tell him that the client had arrived and that my team was all set to begin. While I was relaying the information, he regarded me, squinty eyed, the way you take in someone you think you know, but aren't quite sure.

"There's something different. Did you change your? No, it's not the hair."

Then he stepped back to give me the full body sweep with his what's-wrong-with-this-picture eyes.

*Oh, Christ, let's just get this over with.* "I put some weight back on."

You would have thought I'd said I'd joined a cult and drank the Kool-Aid.

"Why, yes you have."

I refused to let this man's accusatory face make me feel bad. Only on perhaps, Planet Anorexia in the galaxy known as Bulimia would I be considered fat.

"I was warned that I'd gotten too thin so I changed my exer…"

"Yes, yes. Can't keep the client waiting. Shall we?"

And I was hustled out the door.

By interrupting so much, Craig cut short the presentation preamble that was my responsibility to give. Before I knew it, it was time for Byron's creative dog and pony. And what a show he put on. The client was beaming, therefore Craig was beaming, and Byron, yes, he beamed too.

I was happy for him – all decked out in black Hugo Boss with dark blue shirt and gray tie. He had seen the ensemble when we covered a fashion shoot the magazine was doing as part of the "Behind-the-Scenes" campaign. He begged the stylist to let him buy the clothes right off the model's back, but was told they were not for sale and had to be returned to the designer. But Byron has a way, so by the end of the day he owned the outfit, which the designer let him have for free because, "My young British friend is such a devoted fan." Byron promised he'd be photographed in it when GQ did the (only in his dreams) profile of him.

It was my turn again to talk "numbers." The Silver Fox, however, had other ideas. He stood up and said slyly, "Byron is on a roll. Why doesn't he just continue?"

I was a bit confused, but there was no time to dwell, and it was certainly not the place to argue. I handed the meeting over to my colleague.

Unprepared to go it alone, Byron took center stage with a smile that said "yes, yes" but there was "oh no" in his eyes as he looked my way. I winked to show I had every confidence that his inner Jackson Heights would kick in and he would just go with it.

With me by his side, Byron and his *faux* King's English jumped into the presentation.

"OK, let's begin with, oh, um...I think Trish, maybe you could just read the data before I..." then he caught himself when he caught the glare in Craig's eye. That man did not want me to say a word. And I was fighting my suspicion as to why, so I could maintain my team player demeanor.

I took the paper from which I was planning to reference the anticipated rise in subscribers, increase in circulation and other statistics, and before Craig could pull a move from the past and snatch it from my hand to pass it to Byron, I gave it to him myself with a helpful smile. It had been a while, but I still knew that drill all too well.

"Great," Byron said as he cleared his throat, "well, the target spends almost 60 percent of their income..."

He didn't know what he was talking about but, I must admit, he sounded authoritative just the same. Ah, the powers of sounding like one hails from the Mother Country.

# Chapter 27

## "Gaining It Back"

The next morning, I arrived at the ghost town that was usually my hyper-drive agency. I noticed that Craig, Byron and most of our staff were not in their offices. I stopped Craig's secretary as she walked efficiently back to her desk from his office.

"Darlene, where is everybody?" I asked casually.

"Out," she answered nervously.

"Out where?" Thinking that my mimicking was more funny than rude.

She didn't. That's why Darlene decided to put me in my place with, "Out at the meeting."

"What meeting?"

I had once had root canal that was not as painful as getting a straight answer from this woman.

She took a deep breath. Her eyes closed in the way they teach you at self-actualization meetings. I could tell she was doing some self-talking, something along the lines of *I will answer calmly. None of this is my fault. I'm only the messenger.*

"The *TREND* meeting," she said succinctly, while she shuffled papers and arranged pens in the Image mug she used as a pencil holder, so that she wouldn't have to make eye contact. Then she paused, as if daring me to yell at her. I didn't. I took an even deeper breath than she had. Darlene had returned to trying to man the phones and keep straight both Craig's business and personal calendars. I think she thought I would just go (*aka* storm) away and slam my door.

I placed my hand over the calendar page on the computer screen she was checking, which forced her to look back in my face. She pursed her lips and was so mortified at my intrusive gesture that I knew she'd be happy to hurt me and spill the beans when I asked, "What *TREND* meeting?"

Lisa was out at the Hanes client, so with no one to share my latest career blow, I hid in my office with the door closed, until around four when my bladder almost exploded.

I stood at the sink washing and re-washing my hands as if I had an obsessive-compulsive disorder. I thought I was in there alone, until I heard a flush. I looked up into the mirror past my own reflection to witness the ever perfect Chelsea emerging from one of the stalls like a Monarch butterfly from its chrysalis.

Her hair was even blonder, ever longer, even silkier than I had remembered. Her suit was Donna Karan, worn without a shirt so a hint of spray-tanned boobage could be spied from just the right angle.

"You're baaaaack?" My horrified shriek gave the impression that I was talking to a poltergeist. I tried to recover my loss of control with a more professional, matter-of-fact tone, "I mean, you're back."

Too late. She was already savoring my panicky state.

"Well, we'll see. I'm just consulting at the moment." She said this as she admired herself in the mirror, never giving me the courtesy of looking at me even once.

"Really? On what?" Pretending even to myself that I didn't know.

Chelsea grinned in that Nicolette-Sheridan-Desperate-Housewives-I-stole-your-man way. Then one of the subordinates on the *TREND* account walked in.

"Hi Trish. Hey, Chelsea, great meeting."

*Well, that answered that.*

"Yes. Thanks." She said to the wide-eyed newbie even though she was finally looking in my face. Then, Chelsea sashayed out.

I pulled rank and demanded the underling cough up the details. Fearing for her job (and perhaps her life), out they came. Apparently, the team, *sans* me, was called at home last night by Craig and told to meet at *TREND* to reintroduce Chelsea to the client. He told them that although I'd been a valued player, her experience as a model would really add that extra something to the final product.

"And the client…?" I asked.

According to the underling, Craig's usual nonsensical double-talk worked its magic.

It was a good thing we were having our conversation in the bathroom, since I thought I might wet myself.

Without so much as a, "Thanks for the heads up," I left the ladies room. With purpose in every step, I took the many twists and turns towards the monster corner office, the whole time reminding myself to be calm. *You'll get nowhere if you pitch a fit.* Plus it will only make Chelsea look more in control and poised – someone who management would actually want to put in front of the client. Explain that if he's decided to let her back on *TREND*, well, it's his agency. But, we have to be co-leaders on the account. *I will not report to her*.

I reached Craig's doorway, and as though I were a prospective client in need of a good schmooze, he ballyhooed, "Trish, just the person I wanted to see."

# Chapter 28

## "The Skinny"

"Toilette Fresh?" Lisa screamed in a whisper as I shut her door.

I hadn't spoken to anyone right after my humiliating meeting with Craig. I had walked confidently back to my office so that no one would suspect I had just been demoted. I mean I was still a VP Account Supervisor, but on a lesser account. And I will confess, I was only human and made a pit stop in the lobby and used my additional ten daily POINTS on two bags of M&Ms – one plain; one with peanuts.

Once I got into my office, I felt the dam about to burst. I could not risk that someone might walk in and see me blubbering, so I decided to take the rest of the day off.

I kept it together all the way down the hallway as I gave a "see, all-is-right-in-my-world" wave to my colleagues toiling away at their desks. I wasn't going to make it to the elevators though, so I ducked in to see Lisa and let 'er rip.

"You should have heard him," I told her. "He made it sound like it was a promotion. 'Oh Trish, you've already worked wonders with *TREND*. They don't need you anymore. Now it's all hand holding. That's why I brought Chelsea back'."

"Ah, nothing like bullshit served up on a Silver platter," sneered Lisa.

"Then he says, 'TF desperately needs your help .'"

"Did you call him on the secret meeting?"

"I was afraid," I had to admit with my head down.

"Afraid he'd fire you for putting him on the spot?" Lisa tried to clarify.

"Yeah." No. I could not say aloud, even to my friend, that I feared that even if I assured him that my weight gain was merely a way of reaching a healthier place – as opposed to the first stop on the Porky Express – that he would not believe me. This would be yet another reminder that my dad, the one man who would have believed me because he believed in me, was no longer here.

When I was as composed as I was ever going to get, Lisa did reconnaissance for me, checking the hall, waiting until the coast was clear so she could shoo me into the elevator. Once inside, I distracted myself by intensely watching the floor numbers decrease as though I could will them to speed it up. As I stepped out of the building's revolving door and onto the always-crowded sidewalk, I competed as I never had before with other New Yorkers also trying to hail a taxi.

I beat to a cab someone with a leg cast who had flagged the yellow prize down with his crutch. I believe I heard the word "bitch" bandied about by him and other pedestrians as we drove off.

"You all right, Miss?" asked the cabby.

I started crying so hard right after I had blurted out my address that I could not answer. I was hoping that he just thought that I did not hear him, but I'm sure he thought he had picked up yet another rude fare.

When we reached my building, still unable to speak without hiccupping or slobbering, I gave him a generous tip in the hope of redeeming myself.

Another time and place, I would have had a nice long heart-to-heart with Ben & Jerry, who would remind me that life's a Rocky Road, but this night I hopped on my stationary bike and pedaled as though it was going to take me to a galaxy far, far away.

It was now clear that like so many things in my life, my professional world needed an overhaul. I would never change The Silver Fox or what had transpired that day, so I had to figure out what I could do.

I remembered how in grammar school I would come home and tell my father things like how Sister Cranky Pants had singled me out during the Spelling Bee and sniped, "Miss Collins, why don't you spell for us the word 'insouciant' since that is what you are."

He would first agree with me that her words were indeed not very nice, then say, "Now, my girl, tell me what part you played in all this."

"Nothing," would be my first line of defense. Then, he would look at me with his bright eyes, an arched eyebrow, and smile a conspiratorial "come on you can tell me" smile and I would spill: Perhaps it was the way I stood there with my arms folded across my chest, rolling my eyes, while huffing and puffing like the Big Bad Wolf gearing up to blow down the straw house of the first Little Pig. Or maybe it was my attempts to make eye contact with my home girl, Eileen McLaughlin, so that we could make faces in unison at the lameness that is The Bee. In essence, I was insouciant.

Now, I had to look in the mirror and challenge myself: "So my girl, what part did you play in all this?"

I knew from the get-go that Craig Silver, albeit an ad legend in his own time, was a not very nice, unfair, user, yet I took the job and stayed anyway because I loved the cachet of working for a star whose agency was the gold standard.

And I had been more than a loyal Image employee. I'd allowed myself to become a slave to the idea that this great man had had mercy and chosen me, the sometimes fat, sometimes skinny, little fatherless girl from the Bronx, to work in the presence of his greatness.

As I got off my bike, I was not only sweaty and panting, but relieved that my days of *Craig wants... Craig needs... Craig says...* were numbered. I would begin to search for a new job.

The next day, my first assignment as the VP of Toilette Fresh was to call several headhunters, who must have all been reading from the same HR manual. "You want to get hired in fourth quarter? Good luck. People are just getting into holiday mode. Let's talk in the New Year."

The old me would have let her emotions get the best of her and subsequently taken a nose-dive into a vat of corn chips and whatever else I could have scrounged up in the agency's kitchen cupboard. But not this time.

I hated admitting this, but I wished I could have been like Chelsea and up and left in a huff. I mean, I had savings and was fully vested in the company so I could have been OK financially for at least six, maybe eight months. But that's not my way. I'd come from a long line of hard working blue-collar people who instilled in me a sense of pride in having a job, any job. And for as long as you had it, it was worth doing well. "Go big or go home," as my dad used to say.

So for as long as I was still there, I would not only do my job in a big way, but try and project a positive outlook about my new account.

After all, this product had been around since indoor plumbing had been invented. It was number one in the bathroom cleaning products category. And it generated more money than Coke and Pepsi combined. Apparently, everyone wants a clean toilet above all else and Toilette Fresh truly worked the best.

But for once, it wasn't cash that kept the business at the agency. It was loyalty. TF, as Craig called it, so he wouldn't have to say the word "toilet", had been the account that had helped him launch Image.

That said, everyone, I think even the client, knew he was embarrassed to have them on our client roster and delegated the chore of running that piece of business to those he didn't think much of.

"Have you spoken to Byron?" Lisa wanted to know after she meandered into my office looking for some file she knew I wouldn't have.

I bristled.

"No, I have not spoken to 'my friend' Byron."

Lisa gave me a look like c'mon, is it his fault?

Then before I could answer, there was a knock on the door and Byron entered before hearing anyone say, "Come in."

"Girrrrrl." He addressed me, Brit accent-free.

"Thanks pal." I knew it was unfair to blame him, but I said it anyway.

"Shit, Patricia, what did you want me to do? Title or no title, I'm just a cog in the wheel, like everybody else."

"Enough," Lisa commanded, "from the both of you."

"I'm sorry baby, but…" Byron started to say with outstretched arms.

I fell into them and gave a perfunctory hug. I just wanted to move on.

My power of positive thinking was in full swing until I heard a commotion in the hallway. I looked up from my spreadsheet and saw *TREND*-worthy Chelsea along with *bon vivant* Byron walking down the hall.

He glanced casually around and saw me watching. I waved to show I had no hard feelings – at least towards him.

Byron told me once that he could have easily gone the other way. "I'd be in jail right now, with the rest of the homeboys from my 'hood."

After his older brother got sent away, and he saw the despair and anguish on the faces of his mother and grandmother, he decided he never wanted to cause them or anyone that kind of disappointment or pain.

So Brian from Queens became Byron from a country that has a queen, used his finely honed street-hustler ways to charm a newly minted employment agency recruiter from Minnesota to get him a job in a good company. She came up with the mailroom at a major ad agency.

From there, Byron sought out the only black Creative Director in the whole place and worked his urban version of Blanche Dubois. "I've always depended on the kindness of strangers."

The guy reached out to "his young brother" and made Byron his assistant (secretary actually, but By liked the sound of assistant better.) At first Byron, who barely finished high school and had no real command of English grammar or punctuation, took the initiative and started writing copy on his own, showed it to the seasoned pros around the office, incorporated their suggestions, then showed his boss, never bothering to mention his collaboration with other staff members.

The impressed Creative Director began giving Byron his own copy assignments; then after about a year and a half, promoted him to junior copywriter.

When Byron had enough samples in his portfolio, he kissed his mentor goodbye, donned his best designer-sample sale clothes and landed at Image as a Creative Supervisor. He billed himself as "an idea man" and left the actual writing to those below him. This obviously was the right move, because there he was, the VP Creative Director for the *TREND* Magazine account.

I was happy that my colleague had not “gone the other way.” I was pleased that someone’s dream had come true.

## Chapter 29

### "Objects In The Mirror… "

The next morning, I was introduced to the hefty, bald, sixty-ish, and crusty Toilette Fresh client.

He reminded me of a bulldog. Not just because his face was all pushed in, but also because he seemed like he was always ready for a fight. His bring-it-on demeanor made him gruff and aggressive when there was really no need to be; after all, we had direct orders from Craig to give Mr. T.F. whatever he wanted. But he always barked, even when he was saying "Thank you" – which he hardly ever said – except for that first day to the secretary who fetched him his coffee: black, five sugars. *Well, if he couldn't be sweet on the outside…*

By way of introduction, he kept it simple. There was such a great agency turnover on this account that he didn't want to have to waste time on some longwinded speech every few months.

"I've worked for this company for forty years. I'd drink the stuff if they asked me to. You just do as I say and we'll all get along just peachy. Got it?"

I'm sure there was an appropriate response to his admission of loyalty to this cleaning and disinfecting agent, which perhaps quintessential ad man, Don Draper, would have come up with on the fly. I just sort of nodded my head and stared trying to look serious and interested, as opposed to amused and slightly sickened at the thought of that smelly, blue, ammonia-fueled fluid as a light beverage.

"If you're going to be heading up my business, you have to understand the true importance of the fresh smelling toilet."

I added a smile to my head-nod-stare repertoire, and strived with every fiber of my being not to snicker at the word "importance."

I have had two weeks go by faster than that two-hour meeting went, where Mr. Toilette Fresh spoke of deodorizing the toilet for the consumer so they would never have to fear a guest using their facilities, and cleansing agents that allowed the consumer to scrub less. Never before had I ever been in a meeting, or had a conversation even, where the words "waste," "elimination," or "urine" played such an active role. "Mildew" and "residue" also were used more than I had needed them to be.

From that moment on, I began laboring as "Lady of the Loo," a self-mocking name I gave to myself, before someone else could come up with one less charming.

# Chapter 30

## "Losses and Gains"

The New Year brought the disappointing news that the job market was still slow, unless I wanted to quit my job and consult. "People don't want to pay insurance, and all that," said my favorite headhunter. "They want someone to come in, fix the problem and go."

Freelance always seemed a little too precarious for me, so I just figured I'd hang on and hang in with Toilette Fresh until something else permanent came along.

A couple of weeks later, it was my 30th birthday. Feeling a little low with no man and an oh-no of a job, I chose to celebrate without fanfare, just a simple lunch with my mother at Saks, where she presented me with my "gift."

"My jeans from high school? I can't believe you saved those. You hated them. 'You really can't tell they're jeans under all those patches,' you used to say. 'You look like a hillbilly. A migrant farm worker would have too much pride to wear those pants', I believe were your exact words."

Now she was saying, "But you loved them."

"These were from my post-grapefruit diet or was it the Scarsdale diet, whatever, hippie-chick period."

"I came across them when I was going through some old things. That look is back. You can wear them now," Mother said.

"Nah."

"Oh, c'mon. We can sneak into a dressing room and you can try them quick. It'll be too funny to see you in them again."

*Well, here we go.* "They won't fit."

"But you're skinny now. These look like they could be a size zero."

"I've moved up a size or two."

And there it was – the cult/Kool-Aid face. "Oh, Patricia, not again." She looked so exhausted, and aged ten years right there before my eyes. My mother may not have literally gained and lost the weight with me over the last decade and a half, but I guess just watching me ride the yo-yo had been equally as draining.

"Remember, you even said I looked too thin. I'd taken the dieting and exercise too far. I was under... the people at Weight Watchers have this chart... I need to gain..."

"You're going to Weight Watchers to gain weight? Only you, Patricia. Only. You."

What was I thinking? She wasn't even listening. I was trying and actually succeeding at finding balance with my outside as well as my inside – but of course, there was one area where that just couldn't happen.

"Oh Christ, I can't, I just can't...I can't..."

I got up and left her and my non-traveling pants sitting there. Me: 3-0. Mom: 0.

## Chapter 31

### "Not Of Equal Weight"

It was time for me to preside over this year's new ad campaign presentation to Mr. Toilette Fresh.

Craig was supposed to attend, but only stopped by to make his apologies to the client about some family emergency he had to rush off to handle. The emergency was probably lunch with his wife or side-by-side massages with his mistress. That would be the day that The Silver Fox sat through a meeting about toilet cleanser.

Be that as it may, the show (with neither dog nor pony) had to go on. I began the meeting by presenting him with what I felt was a new and innovative marketing plan, one that broke out of their traditional mold and included avenues, like the internet and creating a MySpace page, to attract new, younger customers. To be honest, I had done this not so much for him, but for myself. It kept me sane, busy and made me feel as though I was earning my money.

When I was done, I handed him a bound copy of my ideas that he could bring back to his superiors for discussion. No sooner did he have it in his hand, did he toss it back across the table at me. I was pretty sure he wasn't initiating a game of knock-hockey. "You don't..."

"No," he belched, "I don't." Then he motioned impatiently, making circles with his hand to get on with it.

The television commercial presented by the burned-out and dejected I-only-do-this-crap-so-I-can-support-my-real-writing-I'm-a-novelist-you-know copywriter haunted me for the rest of the day.

The idea had been to do testimonials. Each vignette had a person standing in her bathroom talking about how clean and fresh it smelled. As though on a loop, over and over, all I could hear in my head long after the meeting adjourned was the writer's dulcet monotone voice.

"My rose garden doesn't smell as good as my Toilette Fresh toilet," pounded in my brain, as I came out of Starbucks and saw Chelsea and Byron leading the *TREND* client into Da Silvano for lunch.

I was preoccupied by "Well, my just-diapered baby doesn't smell as good as my Toilette Fresh toilet," as I entered my building and the doorman handed me my dry cleaning.

I was losing my mind to the tune of, "Steaks sizzling on the grill don't smell as good as my Toilette Fresh toilet," when I walked into my apartment, dropped down to the floor, sat against the door and began to cry, to the kicker announcer line, "See, everyone agrees. Nothing smells quite as good as a toilet flushed with Toilette Fresh."

## Chapter 32

### "Scaling Back"

Before I had a chance to make my daily round of morning calls to my many recruiters, Darlene phoned to summon me. *Craig wants...Craig says... Craig needs...*

"I'm off the account?" No, no, no, no, no, I shrieked to myself while I imagined wagging a defiant index finger in my boss's face, right before I used it and the one next to it to deliver a Three Stooges eye poke.

I was supposed to reject Mr. Toilette Fresh, not the other way around. He was lucky I stayed on the business as long as I had.

"'What does she really do anyway?' were his exact words that, by the way, he shouted in my office after the meeting." Craig sighed, as though I should apologize for the inconvenience. "He figured between himself and the creative team, the work would get done and any administrative stuff could be handled by a lower-level account person who didn't cost as much. This conversation, of course, happened after I was forced to spell out for him what MySpace is."

I thought, after all my loyal service to the agency and its clients, Craig would have come to my defense with, "Trish is a smart, hardworking executive with high standards in her life and her work. I should never have let her be associated with an account that truly belongs in the toilet."

In reality, he said the words that from the beginning of his career secured his and his agency's place in advertising history, "You're the client. Whatever you want."

I took a deep breath and said, "Fine. So, what account do you want me to service now?"

After I was "released" (only The Silver Fox could make being fired sound so lyrical), I remained composed, said I was disappointed in his decision, thanked him for the opportunity to have worked there, then went back to my office to call the only headhunter whom I knew could help me.

"I'm finally ready to take the plunge, quit my job and give consulting a go." *OK*, I thought to myself, *at least you're not a "fat" liar*.

Lisa and I, holding a box of my office paraphernalia (the rest would be messengered), stood at the curb.

"There's one," Lisa said, as she held up her hand like a crossing guard and the yellow taxi screeched to a halt.

He graciously popped the trunk without being told and I loaded my possessions.

"Well, I'll call you," I assured Lisa.

As we hugged, she supported me with "Freelance might be a nice change – for a while, until... It's for the best. I know you'll find a new job that actually suits you," she said with the certainty of someone who did not have to go looking for employment.

Still trying to at least appear positive, I said, "I know I will, too."

I got in the cab and stuck my head out the window. "I may never flush my toilet again, but I will find a new job."

## Chapter 33

### "Thin-skinned"

"Hello."

"Ma, it's me."

"Patricia," my mother said in that way Jerry Seinfeld's character Jerry used to address Newman.

"I just wanted you to know that at present I have lost my job and also do not have one solid relationship in my life with a man, but I'm proud to say that for once I am dealing with it by not stuffing myself with food as you taught me to do after my father was taken from me, which I realize was out of anyone's control, but you should have brought me to therapy or given me support in other ways than as to shove food in my face."

So there. I spewed that self-righteousness mouthful of the truly stupid, who allow every piece of ignorance that pops in their head to fall out their mouth – with pride no less.

"I see."

"And, furthermore," I began. (Yes, I was on a roll. Because when a grown woman is acting like a two-year-old, seriously, why stop?) "My father was everything to me, and I was just a young girl when I lost him and even though he could never be replaced, you tried to replace my feeling for him my filling me up with lasagna and a 'nice piece of cake'."

"Are you done?"

Was she kidding? This was just the beginning. "Then, after you fattened me up, you brought me down with your insults about not looking nice."

Finally, it was out. I had put it out there so she could see what she had done to me. She could finally take responsibility for her behavior, which did me irreparable harm. Yes, let the apologies begin, although no amount of groveling on her part could change my resentments towards her.

But post-tirade, there was silence. Such a long one in fact, that I thought she had hung up on me.

"Mom? Ma? You there?"

"He was everything to me, too," she said, with what I believed was the slightest hint of you idiot in her tone. "When he died, we had just celebrated our Silver Wedding Anniversary – twenty-five years. We'd been married twelve years before you came along. I thought I wasn't able to have children." She said she used to cry because she felt so disappointed that she had not given my father a family. She told me he would hold her and say, "A baby would be wonderful, but as long as I have you... "

I started to cry, but covered my mouth so no sobs could escape. I wanted her to keep talking, although I was not sure I could bear it.

"I told him once I would follow him anywhere. The day he was killed I wanted to follow him to heaven. Do you know what I'm saying Patricia?"

"Um... " It was hard for me to even imagine my mother as suicidal.

"Yeah, um. And I would have done it, but I had to keep living because I had a child to care for. I did the best I could, but sometimes, well, my best was to just make it through the day. I guess we could have afforded therapy, but quite frankly, our kind of people, you know, regular people didn't do that. We just muddled through."

I had to keep looking at the phone. I don't know why. It's not like I could see her or anything to verify that I was indeed speaking to my mother. She had never opened up to me before. Now she was the one on a roll.

"And I couldn't talk about it or listen to you talk about it. I couldn't listen to your pain or sadness because I was afraid mine would overcome me and I really would end it all. So to keep you from sharing how much you missed him, I put something in your mouth. Then it just became a habit, whether you had a problem with a boy or a friend or school. I'm sorry. I'm sorry I did that to you, but I had to save myself."

I thought about that last statement and had to admit, I was glad she saved herself.

"But you just kept eating, Patricia." *My girl, what part did you play in this?* "I may have given you 'a nice piece of cake'," she said, mocking my mock of her, "but I never told you to eat the whole cake. When I would see what was happening to you, I appealed to the only thing that matters to girls at that age, 'Do I look nice, so I'll attract boys?' "

What else could I say? My mother believed she had done the right thing. Me being me, I'm sure I could have kept arguing, accusing, blaming... but, I was as tired of that as I had become of watching the scale fluctuate. If I really wanted to achieve balance, total balance inside and out, I had to accept that she had done the best she could, and then once and for all, just let it all go. I can't really explain it, but just deciding to take the action, made me feel a whole lot lighter than any diet I had ever been on.

"I think it's time we just start remembering the good times."

She agreed. "Now what's this about the job?"

I could no longer hide my sniffling. "I need to talk about that another time. I um, I need to go. I'll call, tomor... soon."

With that, I sat to digest all my mother had said. I believe I lay there on my sofa for about three days, getting up only to go to the bathroom and of course, to get something to eat.

# Chapter 34

## "Weight of the World"

"There must be some line at the bakery," my mother said to me as we waited longer than usual for my father to return.

I didn't bother to respond because the bell rang. I got up from the sofa, sort of pissed that my dad had forgotten his key and I actually had to trouble myself to move.

I flung open the door. "What took…oh. Hi," I said to the young policeman, whom I figured was a friend of my father's, since his bar attracted a lot of cops and fireman.

"My dad's not here."

"Is your mommy home?"

This guy could not have been more than six or seven years older than me, yet he was talking to me like I was a pre-schooler. To let him know how much I did not appreciate that, I gave him my best pre-teen sneer and said, "Sure, my ma-mee's home. Let me go get her." Then I let go of the door, so that he'd either have to stop it with his hand or his black Oxfords to keep it from slamming in his face.

My behind had just taken its rightful place back on the sofa cushion, when my mother let out a scream, and I heard what sounded like a sack of potatoes hit the vestibule floor.

"I need an ambulance, forthwith, at...," Officer Rookie was shouting into his walkie-talkie.

I shot up and saw my mother lying on the floor and under my breath I started chanting, "Daddy, Daddy, Daddy, where are you?"

When he did not miraculously appear out of thin air like Barbara Eden on *I Dream of Jeannie*, I ran past my dead mother and the policeman who was trying to revive her, out the door, down three flights (in one jump it seemed like) out onto the street and down the block. I knocked on the door of our family physician, who lived two buildings down from us in the ground floor apartment.

He opened the door with his thinning white hair uncombed, still holding the *Sunday New York Daily News*, to hear me yell, "My mother is dead!" Then I ran outside and back up the block to my house.

By the time I arrived, Dr. Wynn was right behind me in his trousers, black leather house slippers and white undershirt, and was holding his medical bag, which he must have had handy and grabbed on his way out.

Officer Rookie had managed to revive my mother; however, she was hysterical and incoherent. With EMS quickly approaching our front door, the doctor combed his hair back with his fingers trying to attain his office-hours look and demanded to know, "What the hell happened?"

As the inexperienced policeman blurted out the unthinkable, Dr. Wynn, who had actually been a friend of my father's, and whose professional training had supposedly prepared him to handle the unthinkable, threw his hands up to his now beet-red face and spit, "Jesus H. Christ."

Well, if even the doctor was going to lose it, what chance did I have? Without consulting me, my body fell up against the living room wall, dropped to the floor, and I began to sob uncontrollably, as well as shake and rock back and forth screaming, "No!"

The players may have changed, but one thing remained the same. I was still shy one parent.

The doctor was in the middle of instructing the cop to go upstairs and get my Aunt Emma, but she was already on her way down to see what the hubbub was all about. Everything sounded as though it was happening a million miles away, but I believe I heard a bloodcurdler come out of her, too.

Large and in charge, even in his bedroom slippers, Dr. Wynn sent the EMS guys away after they and the officer helped him carry my mother into what was now just her bedroom, all the while instructing my aunt to "calm down and take care of the girl," and at the same time directing the super, who materialized in our entrance hall as if by *Star Trek* transporter, to, "get these people out of here," referring to the neighbors who had gathered outside our door to find out what was going on, some even spilling across the threshold into our apartment. It was like being in an episode of *M.A.S.H.*

The rest of the day was a blur because it was seen through a steady stream of tears.

*************

Before my father left that morning, he looked at me, and put his index finger over his lips so I would not give away his freshly showered presence. He then snuck up behind my mother, who was standing at the kitchen counter reading the paper. He squeezed her shapely waist, nuzzled her olive neck and kissed her smooth cheek, which rose to meet his lips.

She squeaked with surprise, then, laughed with her head back, her eyes closed and her bow mouth wide open, begging him to stop because he was tickling her.

That was the last time I ever saw my mother genuinely happy.

# Chapter 35

## "Lightening The Load"

By the end of day three, and in the middle of twirling my fork around the noodles in my Lean Cuisine Fettucini Alfredo, came my epiphany. I realized that I had always overeaten to fill the void left not by my father, but by my mother.

When I lost my him, I lost her too. The only man she had ever loved had been taken from her in a violent, careless way. He didn't even die in a bed on clean sheets. His deathbed was a dirty New York City street.

How had she not lost her mind? Feeding me was clearly not the only thing she did to save herself. She turned the emotion switch to off. I guess, if she didn't feel, she wouldn't hurt.

With that, the connection between us was gone, and I spent the rest of my childhood, and life thus far, hungering for the sweet comfort only a mother can give. I discovered that sweetness and comfort in the form of candy and chocolate, jelly donuts and the kind with glaze and sprinkles on top, and lest we forget, ice cream.

From birth, we depend on this one person to feed us both physically and mentally. She's the only human on the planet who can perform both tasks.

As a grown woman, I sat with my girlhood's gnawing hunger for her affection stored up inside me. I realized that I ate to taste her unconditional love so I would eventually feel lovable. But all I ever felt was bloated.

About a week later, when I had made peace with my new view of my mother, I called her back as I had said I would.

"Hello?"

"I'm sorry, too," I announced hoping she would remember that I was picking up our conversation where she had left off.

"Patricia?"

"I couldn't have known as a little girl what you were going through, but now, as a grown woman... does it still cause you pain to talk about it?"

"Yes."

I was disappointed to hear that. She had closed herself up again. If she spoke to me, I might be able to help her now. Or I could get her help. But, I asked the question and got a very definitive answer. I chose to respect it.

"Then we won't," I said. "I understand."

It was official. I had forgiven my mother. It was not her fault that her husband died and that she couldn't deal with it. She had done better than many people would have fared in her position – including me.

To her credit, she always did her motherly duties. She used the double indemnity payment on the insurance policy, and the sale of the bar, (there was a bidding war due to the prime Kingsbridge Road and Jerome Avenue location), to send me to good schools, made sure I had clean clothes, and it goes without saying, put food on the table.

She kept her position at the phone company to keep herself distracted, not to mention alive, so she would have the where-with-all to get up every day to take care of me. But, after using all her energy to do her many jobs, there wasn't much left over for "mothering."

I'd been starved for her affection since adolescence, and it was probably too late to ask this aging woman, who was set in her ways, to become a different kind of mother. So, unless I wanted to continue to be a starved adult, I would have to learn to mother myself.

## Chapter 36

### "Worth The Weight"

Consulting was better (translation: less anxiety producing) than I anticipated, even though every place I worked, people just had to ask the proverbial question, "What's The Silver Fox really like?"

I had worked at Image for so long that I started to feel as though I'd been "released" from prison. It was refreshing to not be tied down to a job, yet still get a paycheck. I even picked up a new friend here and there, and had a number of nice lunch dates. No one with relationship potential, but good company just the same.

After a few months though, I was starting to get the itch for permanence. Even though I'd spent my adult life in Greenwich Village, I never really embraced the whole free-spirit thing. As luck, and a brief upswing in the job market would have it, I ended up getting an assignment at a place that really felt like home.

I guess they felt the same way about me. That and a glowing recommendation from Lisa, who had been promoted to SVP at Image, secured the offer.

I shook hands with the EVP Account Manager of the world's third largest ad agency as he tendered the ever-hokey, but nevertheless sincere, "Welcome aboard."

As soon as I settled into my new job as VP Account Supervisor at a place that appreciated my range of experience, everyone started to buzz about the company's upcoming annual summer kick-off party.

I wanted something new for the event, so I went to Saks.

A saleswoman approached, took my selections and said, "Here, let me start a room for you."

I held up a pair of slacks wanting to know, "Are these the last pair?"

"Oh no. We have more in the back. Let's see," she said checking the tags on my garments. "Yes, we have your size. We always run out of the really small and really large sizes first."

I guess I wasn't the only one whose weight had ever landed them on opposite ends of the spectrum.

Finally though, I had actually moved right to the middle of the healthy weight range indicated on that handy-dandy Weight Watchers chart, and that's where I planned to stay.

"Welcome back," said the counselor when I re-upped with the weight loss program (at a different location than the one where I'd embarrassed myself), not just for the monthly stay-the-course weigh-ins, but for the meetings which I attended at least three times a week. Like "friends of Bill W." who find strength from their anonymous sharings, it was good for me to surround myself with those who understood me because they too, had been "friends of Ben & Jerry."

I also added "downward-facing dog" to my lexicon, since a Pure Yoga opened just across the street from my apartment house.

It was Thursday evening, the night before the company-wide four-day Memorial Day Weekend vacay. The bash my new agency threw was a lavish and fun blast from the past held on the rooftop of Hotel Gansevoort in the über-trendy Meatpacking District. There was a live band *à la* The B-52s and the servers were dressed like greasers in leather jackets and bobby-soxers in poodle skirts.

To the tune "Runaround Sue," I walked about chatting with people I had gotten to know in my short time there and introduced myself to those I hadn't.

I headed to the bar and a cute, albeit average looking and thirty-ish, guy sidled up and, like me, waited patiently. The bartender was entertaining a group of young, perky and flirty assistants at the end of his oak podium. Now, I know from bartenders, and this one left a lot to be desired.

Although I never hung out at my dad's place of business, I had been there. I'd drop by to give him something from my mother, or to show him a good report card because I just couldn't wait until he got home. And of course, if there was something to celebrate, his bar is where we'd have the party. More than once, someone had approached me to compliment my father. Not just about his character, but for his skills. "Your ol' man sure knows how to fix a drink."

He was like a magician behind that bar. It was like he could make eight cocktails at once. He would field drink orders from opposite ends of the bar from ten different people and get all of them right. He would have put this rent-a-barman to shame.

To pass the time, I kept sneaking peeks in the mirror behind the bar at the cute guy, whom I knew had to be a colleague. Standing there next to him and not saying anything was awkward. So I smiled. He smiled back.

Suddenly, I forgot I was at a business function and felt weirdly self-conscious. Did my hair look OK? Was my lipstick still on?

What was I thinking? This guy wasn't even my type. Wait, did I have a type? My ex-fiancé had been a singer in what turned out to be a One-Hit-Wonder rock band. Kevin was a permanent-press preppy. Rick, a strapping he-man. This guy was...scruffy. Scruffy in a GQ way – jeans and a classic Ralph Lauren white button-down with a navy jacket. He wasn't clean cut, but he wasn't Shaggy from Scoobie-Doo either. In fact, he had a mass of beautiful dark brown waves I really wanted to run my fingers through.

I had spent my dating life trying to replace a man I had loved when I was a little girl. Even though I had never found a man like my dad, I think I was attracted to each of my exes because he had exhibited at least some trait in common with him.

The rocker had been creative. My dad was a great storyteller. Some stories were wise, others funny. But it was his gift for telling that held everyone's attention. Kevin had been hardworking and very attached to his family; my dad was a good provider and his motto was "Family First." Rick was down to earth; my dad was called, "salt of the earth," by the priest who said the mass at his funeral and the throngs in attendance all nodded in unison. And back in high school, Tommy Kelly, well, he was the cutest guy in our neighborhood. My mother would say of my dad, "He is one beautiful man," when she would see him turn the corner and walk up the block on his way home from work.

Perhaps though, it was time I looked for a man I could love as the woman I now was.

"He looks a little like John Cusack," I would eventually tell Lisa.

"So what's a girl gotta do to get a drink around here?" he blustered as if on my behalf.

"I don't know, but if I want to drink it in our lifetime, I better order something simple. The *Sex & the City* wannabe's are getting Pink Squirreled or Dirty Martinied shaken not stirred."

"No, no. They drink Cosmopolitans," he mocked on.

"Whatever. You get the picture and it's taking forever," I said.

He extended his hand. "Rob Thompson."

"Trish Collins."

"Oh, right. I got the memo. You're the new VP, Account Puba."

"I prefer Account Diva. And you are a..."

"VP, Creative Director. I prefer Czar."

A Fonzi look-a-like server strutted over with a platter of *hors d'oeuvres*, of which I allowed myself one.

Rob declined.

"Czars don't eat pigs-in-a-blanket?"

"Hors d'oeuvres to me are like Lays Potato Chips. I can't eat just one. So gotta have none," he said, as though admitting it aloud would keep him from caving.

"Been there."

"I mean, I'm not on a diet or anything, I just don't 'supersize' anymore if you know what I mean. That's enough to let me maintain this Pillsbury Doughboy physique that the chicks really dig."

He poked at his little paunch the way they do in the commercials. I chuckled like the little doughy figure himself.

"I went through this weight training phase," he told me, "where I had the whole six-pack-abs-of-steel-Popeye-forearms thing...but, unless I took a gig as a lifeguard or just walked around shirtless, which by the by, the agency frowns upon, what was the point?"

In an I-can-top-that tone, "I was a size zero."

"Zero?" He pondered for a moment. "So technically you walked around wearing nothing. Sorry you didn't work here then."

"Had a personal trainer, virtually no body fat...only muscle..."

"More powerful than a locomotive...able to bend steel with her bare hands," he added.

Now, how would he handle the whole truth? "Before that, I was the proverbial fat chick."

"So then your butt was more powerful than a locomotive. You'd just sit on the steel and it would bend."

The image of that made me start to laugh. Now it was my turn to amuse him.

"They could have put a string on me and floated me in the Macy's Thanksgiving Day Parade."

"With Snoopy and Miss Piggy."

"My fat ass would have knocked Snoop and Piggy right off Central Park West."

"All the way over the Hudson?" he said to add to the drama.

But I bested him again with, "Honey, we're talkin' all the way across New Jersey."

Score. He was laughing; then trying to act cool, he regained his composure.

"And now you're...looking pretty good from here."

I spied myself in the mirror behind the bar and I liked what I saw.

"From here too. I'm not the fat chick. Not the skinny chick."

"You're the hot chick," chimed in an Elvis-impersonating waiter who offered us some seafoody mush thing that we both declined – no self-control needed; since the delicacies looked as though someone had already chewed them up and spit them out into their endive beds.

"I'm flattered," I told Elvis, "but I like to think of myself as the 'just right' chick."

"Just when I thought I had a nice rap goin' here, I get trumped by The King," said Rob.

I just smiled. I liked him and sensed he liked me. I knew we worked in the same company, (and the adage not to you-know-what where you eat) but we weren't going to actually work together.

My *TREND* experience garnered me a place on the Ann Taylor account, and Toilette Fresh put me in a position to lead some packaged goods clients. Rob was working on soft drinks, snacks and candy. Fun stuff, like him.

"How are you not five hundred pounds from all the product samples you must have in your office?" I needed to know.

"I give it all to my secretary to bring home to her kid, who I understand is ready to be Jenny Craig's first spokeschild."

But enough about him; he really seemed to be interested in me.

"So, what part of the city you live in?" he wanted to know.

"The Upper East Side." As much as my grandmother's apartment had served me well, it had come time for me to move and live where I wanted.

"An uptown girl."

"You're not going to break out into song are you?"

He gestured as though he just might start to belt it out, then stopped. "No. And if you ever heard me sing, you'd be thanking me right now."

"So what do Creative Czars do for fun?" I wanted to know.

"Well, I'd love to say white water rafting, followed up by your basic run of the mill triathlon, but...I like bike riding. Not Lance Armstrong type bike racing or mountain biking...just ridin' around."

"The last bike I rode was..."

"A tricycle?"

"Stationary. It's been quite a while since I rode a real..."

"They say you never forget...buy yourself one – an I-got-a new-job present. I'll even help you pick it out. Around this weekend?" he asked.

"Yeah, but... this weekend?"

"I know. You pegged me as one of those suave weekend-house-in-the-Hamptons guys with his own table at Nick & Toni's," he said trying to keep a straight face, "and you're not totally wrong, of course, but I actually prefer staying in Manhattan during the summer. It clears out. I feel like I own the place. So, you 'round?"

"Actually I am, but... "

"Oh no, you're not one of those 'Rules Girls,' are you? You know, one of the authors of that book got divorced. I guess she didn't follow her own rules."

"I have only one rule: If you don't like what you see, do something about it."

Suddenly, he slapped the bar with both hands then raised them in the air like an evangelical preacher. "Hey wait. 'Just. Do. It.' That should be an advertising slogan."

I was laughing so hard that I had to grab the bar so I wouldn't fall off my stool.

He reached out and caught my elbow as an extra safety net. "So does the fact that I've proven I can entertain you for minutes on end mean that maybe you and I could go somewhere and get a drink sometime? Like tomorrow, after we pick out your bike?"

Now was not the time to explain to him that I had stopped riding bikes after my father got hit by a car. Maybe it was time though to stop using his death to keep alive my "street paranoia."

I did however explain that although I would not be purchasing a bicycle any time soon, I would consider renting one in Central Park and seeing how that went.

I then suggested, "How about we go get that drink now, since apparently we're never going to get served here." I pointed out that the bartender, who my father would have fired by now, was still chatting up the faux Carrie & Co.

"Somewhere quiet where we can talk and get to know one another," he said in earnest.

"Not too quiet. I don't want everyone to turn and stare when you're making me laugh."

No matter what diet I was ever on or how much weight I ever dropped, the one thing I never seemed to lose was the big, boisterous, body-jiggling laugh of a fat chick.

The End

CPSIA information can be obtained at www.ICGtesting.com
Printed in the USA
LVOW130902121112

306926LV00001B/150/P